This book is dedicated to friends, loved ones,
and readers everywhere. I do this for you!

Chapter 1

"YOU'RE REALLY leaving," Blaze said as he sat down in front of Thomas's desk with a sigh. "Why in the hell would you want to do that? This is the land of guys, fun, and a million things to do, all of which will either get you laid or are on the path to getting you laid, and you're going to run back to… where is it exactly you're going?" He leaned forward a little just so Thomas could get a good look at the disbelief in his eyes. "Butt-fuck Egypt?"

Thomas shook his head slowly. "Colorado Springs, and I'm going back home to spend some time with my parents." He growled a little. "Don't you work for me? And since I know you do, why doesn't that insulate me from your whining and bitchiness?" Thomas groused, trying his best to seem upset. He knew it hadn't worked when Blaze simply rolled his eyes.

"Because I'm your best friend, have been since we were in Alpha Chi together, and yeah, you own the company, but you know it wouldn't be anywhere without my sparking personality to help smooth the way for all those deals you've made over the years." Blaze smirked, and Thomas glared at him. "You remember in college we both vowed we were going to make a huge splash in the world, a shitpile of money, and then we were never going to go back to those awful towns where we grew up?" He gave an exaggerated shiver.

Thomas shook his head. "I'm getting tired, Blaze. I built this firm to the point where it has more employees than the high school I attended, and all of them are very smart and know their jobs. Otherwise you and I would never have hired them. I'm only moving back to Colorado Springs, not to the moon, and I'm still going to run the company. I'm just going to do it from a place that's quieter and less… easy."

"Easy! You think New York is easy?" Blaze's eyes widened.

"Yeah, it is. Everything is here for the taking," Thomas countered. "It's too damned easy. There are guys—and girls, if that's your thing—around every single corner. If one won't suffice, just choose another one, or two, maybe three. If you have money, everything seems like it's for sale. And I'm tired of it. Okay? I want something slower." He swallowed and half closed his eyes. "I swear I haven't slept more than a few hours a day in the last eighteen years."

"So you're giving it up," Blaze pressed. "Just like that?"

"My parents are getting older. They haven't said anything, but I know they're going to need help soon.

I want to spend some time with them and maybe build a life."

Blaze nodded. "I know what this is. You're still hurting from when Angus left, and you want to give yourself a change of pace. You know, the best way to get over a man is to find another one, and there are plenty of hot guys in New York who would fall all over themselves for the chance to try to win your heart."

Thomas frowned. Blaze didn't get it. "That's the problem. They're all interested, but I'm not. And for the record, I left Angus. There was nothing between us, and all he did was complain that I worked too much. Everyone I've ever dated has said the same thing: I spent too much time working and not enough time with them."

The desk phone buzzed, and Blaze stood. "That would be Marjorie, and I'm out of here before she sees me sitting with you and decides it would be a good time to tell me all the things I'm doing wrong in my life. Why can't that woman spend her time talking you out of this harebrained idea rather than torturing me?" Blaze tried to look innocent, but Thomas knew he and Marjorie got a perverse thrill out of annoying each other as much as possible.

Thomas waved Blaze off and answered the call.

"Your two o'clock meeting is waiting outside, and your two thirty called and is running a few minutes late. That means your three o'clock is going to be tight and—"

"We'll make it work. We always do." Thomas checked the clock as Blaze hightailed it out of the office. The only good thing about this appointment was that it got him out of talking more with Blaze about

him moving closer to his family. Thomas knew that was going to be a sore subject for Blaze, whose parents had never accepted him for who he was. They still harbored delusions that he'd get over this gay phase of his life, settle down, and produce grandchildren for them. At least Thomas's parents were supportive... even if they drove him a little around the bend.

Thomas stood as his appointment came in, and he motioned toward the conference table. He listened to the proposal, which he really had no interest in, and by the end, he still saw no viable financial benefit for anyone.

He hoped the rest of the afternoon was going to be more productive.

Thankfully it was, and he got plenty done before emerging from his office after seven. Marjorie still sat at her desk, like a gatekeeper. "You don't need to stay this late. Go home and have some fun."

She scoffed, looking at him askance. "This coming from the man who gets here before everyone else and leaves later than most everyone. What are you going to do when you move and you don't have an office to sit in until well into the evening?" She smiled to show him she was only partially kidding.

"I don't know. Are you sure you won't come with me?" He'd already asked her four times, but was willing to try again.

"Yes. I'm sure. I'll hold things down for you here, and once you get to Colorado Springs, I'll help you find an assistant who can work with you there."

Meaning someone who wasn't going to drive Marjorie crazy. She liked things a certain way, and he loved that she was the most organized and efficient

person he'd ever met. Marjorie always thought steps ahead so she could smooth the way and help keep him as efficient as possible. Thomas was going to miss her.

"Everything will be fine, and I'll even stop picking on Blaze… a little."

God, Thomas loved that twinkle in her eyes.

"And once you're gone, I promise to leave the office at five every once in a while."

Thomas chuckled. "Thank you." Leaving her was the one thing that worried him. He depended on her to keep his life organized and together so he could concentrate on the really important things. "Good night. I'll see you in the morning."

"Tomorrow is Saturday, and the movers are coming to start packing your things. I'll send a message to your phone so you don't forget." She smiled and waved as Thomas left the office.

He made it to the elevator before yawning, and leaned against the side of the elevator car for the ride down to the underground parking garage. He told his driver to stop at the bodega on the way home so he could get something to eat. He grabbed something to go and got back into the car for the ride to his apartment.

Thomas went inside and ate his dinner in front of the television, with some papers for company. For years he'd spent his time and energy building Stepford Management into one of the top real estate management and consulting firms in the country. Deal after deal, development after development—he and his teams put them together, brought them to fruition, and made a lot of money doing it. Thomas had more than he could spend now, and he was tired.

He used to look forward to going into the office. When he was younger, deals got him excited and kept him up at night. He used to dream of building towers and filling them with tenants, changing the face of the New York skyline. And he'd done all that. Thomas had worked with some of the biggest and most important people in the city of New York over the years, and he'd loved it. But now the thrill wasn't there anymore. It was just work, and he was self-aware enough to know he needed a change of pace. Something different, slower. He needed a chance to do something other than work.

His phone buzzed in his pocket, and he hauled it out. There was a message from his mother telling him that she seen to it that everything met his requirements and that everything was okay and looked good.

Thanks, Mom, he replied. His mother had taken to texting like a duck to water. She'd always hated talking on the phone, and now she sent messages all the time.

When are you leaving New York?

They're packing things tomorrow. I will fly out Tuesday once I have a few things settled in the office.

Good. The screen indicated that she was still composing a message, so he waited. *Is Marjorie going to come with you?*

No. She's going to stay in New York and organize things here. He set his papers aside and jumped when his phone rang. He certainly hadn't expected his mother to call. "What's up?" he asked.

"Talking might be easier," his mother said with a slight huff. "Are you going to need an assistant here?

Because I'm not going to organize your life for you. That's too much work for an old lady like me."

"You're not old. Marjorie's handling finding an assistant for me." He was so danged tired and not into having this conversation. Marjorie would find him someone he could work well with. It wasn't like he needed someone to work as many hours as she did. He'd still have her to maintain his master calendar and handle the bulk of his needs. Having someone local was a good idea, though.

"Thelma Wilson's grandson just graduated from college and is looking for a job. I told her you were coming and would probably need someone, so I said I'd pass it along."

Great. Just what he needed. His mother trying to find his assistant for him. Thomas was about to tell her that Marjorie would find who he needed, but he wasn't in the mood to argue with his mother. It would get him nowhere and then his mother would be upset. "Have him send his résumé and things to HR in New York. They're handling everything for me." There, that was pretty painless.

"Okay. I'll pass that on to Thelma. Can you tell me the email address he should use?" she asked, and Thomas relayed it. "You travel safe, and call your father and me when you get in." He heard the excitement in her voice. Thomas hadn't been home as much as he probably should have been in the last few years. She and his dad had been delighted when he'd told them he was moving home.

"I will, Mom. You and Dad take it easy, and I'll see you on Wednesday." He got in late on Tuesday and didn't want to disturb them. "Maybe we can have

dinner if you and Dad are free." It was time he slowed down and took the chance to try to build a life that didn't revolve around work.

"There are some nice young men in town, who like other men, and…."

He groaned. Before he came out to his parents, his mother had done her best to fix him up with every eligible girl she knew. Back then he'd made himself busy so he wouldn't have to go on those dates. "Mom, I'm coming home to spend some time with you and Dad. I'm still going to be busy." And the last thing he wanted was his mother picking out men for him. Yes, he was pleased that his parents accepted him for who he was, but his mom playing gay matchmaker was a little over the line. "If I want to date, I will. I'm not some troll who needs his mom to get him dates."

"You be nice," she scolded.

"Then you put away your matchmaking skills and let my love life be." He sighed, because no matter how many times he scolded her, his mother was his mother and was going to do exactly what she liked. "Mess in Collin's love life. He's the straight one, and he's single again." For, like, the third time. She could matchmake with him all she wanted. Lord knew he needed it. "Or better yet, leave us both to figure out our own love lives."

His mom was quiet, and Thomas knew instantly that something was up. "I introduced him to Karla," she confessed sheepishly.

"*You* did that!" he gasped.

"He married her!" Mom protested. "All I did was introduce them. I had no idea she'd turn out to be such a harpy. She was nice when I met her and invited her to dinner."

He rolled his eyes even though she couldn't see it. "That only goes to show that you make a lousy matchmaker. You're too danged nice and you see the good in everyone. I knew that woman was the spawn of Satan two seconds after I met her, but by then she already had that damn ring on her finger and her claws so deep into Collin, it was sickening. All she ever wanted was Collin's money… or what she thought she could extract from me through Collin."

It damn near ruined his relationship with his brother. Karla demanded things—jewelry, a new home—and Collin would try to get them for her. Then, when he couldn't afford it, Collin came to Thomas for money, hat in hand, feeling like a loser. Eventually Thomas stopped the handouts. Collin didn't speak to him for months… until Karla finally left and Collin was out from under her influence. Then and only then did the old Collin start to return.

"I am not a lousy matchmaker. I only make introductions. All I did was invite her to dinner one night. Your brother did the rest." She was getting huffy.

"Still, you have to take some responsibility." If he could get his mother to back off, then he would be in good shape. "Let Collin and me be. We can find partners just fine on our own."

"Fine." She huffed, and Thomas knew she wasn't giving up, only doing a strategic retreat. His matchmaking mother would be back soon enough. "Then should I uninvite the people I have coming over for dinner tonight?"

"Mom. Collin just got divorced three months ago. Let him breathe." For Pete's sake, she moved fast.

"If he doesn't get married to a nice girl soon, they're going to be too old to have kids and I'm never going to be a grandmother." Now the sniffles began, which Thomas knew was his total weakness as far as she was concerned.

"Fine. I'm staying out of this. But if Collin marries another harpy like Karla, I'm holding you responsible." He chuckled when his mother sputtered on the other end of the line. "I'm going to go. You and Dad have a good night." He was about to hang up but paused. "And to say it again, don't you try to fix me up with anyone."

He ended the call, wondering if his mother would listen at all or not. Either way, he was not going to fall for anyone his mother tried to set him up with. He loved her to death, but the woman had bad taste in potential daughters-in-law. Thomas could only imagine the kind of men she'd try to pick out for him. Hell, he'd end up married to his father. The thought made him shudder as he put his phone on the coffee table.

Thomas returned his attention to the papers he'd brought home with him, but quickly realized he was getting nothing done. Setting those things aside, he decided to get some of his personal things packed for the move. Most of the things, he didn't really care about and the movers could take care of. But there were things he didn't want strangers pawing through, so he pulled the suitcases out from under the bed, laid them out, and began filling them with underwear and the clothes he was going to want to take with him on the plane.

He paused at a knock at the door and went to open it.

Blaze breezed into the apartment, looking around. "For God's sake, let me guess—you're packing." He

By ANDREW GREY

Published by DREAMSPINNER PRESS
www.dreamspinnerpress.com

By ANDREW GREY

Published by DREAMSPINNER PRESS
www.dreamspinnerpress.com

Readers love ANDREW GREY

Running to You

"As always Andrew has outdone himself with this story. I urge you to go out and get your copy so you can get lost in Carlos and Billy Joe's world."

—Love Bytes

"Andrew Grey always manages to pull at my heartstrings in so many ways. This book is no exception…"

—Diverse Reader

Smoldering Flame

"Andrew Grey did such an amazing job on this book. It is truly an emotional read."

—Gay Book Reviews

"This is a beautiful story…"

—Paranormal Romance Guild

Buried Passions

"The story blends in interesting themes of prejudice, and not just homophobia. The anti-immigrant sentiment was dealt with in a realistic way. And the Big City versus small town mentality was handled well, too."

—Joyfully Jay

"…this is a well written low angst love story."

—Open Skye Book Reviews

NEW TRICKS

Andrew Grey

Published by
DREAMSPINNER PRESS

5032 Capital Circle SW, Suite 2, PMB# 279,
Taliahassee, FL 32305-7886 USA
www.dreamspinnerpress.com

New Tricks
© 2018 Andrew Grey.

Cover Art
© 2018 Adrian Nicholas.
adrian.nicholas177@gmail.com
Cover content is for illustrative purposes only and any person depicted on the cover is a model.

Mass Market Paperback ISBN: 978-1-64108-068-2
Trade Paperback ISBN: 978-1-64080-632-0
Digital ISBN: 978-1-64080-631-3
Library of Congress Control Number: 2017919801
Mass Market Paperback published December 2018
v. 1.0

Printed in the United States of America
∞
This paper meets the requirements of
ANSI/NISO Z39.48-1992 (Permanence of Paper).

By ANDREW GREY

Published by DREAMSPINNER PRESS
www.dreamspinnerpress.com

put his hands on his hips, glaring at Thomas. "It's a Friday night, the last one you're going to spend in New York for a while." Blaze peered into the bedroom and then back at him. "I knew I had to come save you from yourself. Go back in there and put on some decent clothes. You and I are going out, and we're going to find you some young, hot guy. You might as well leave town with a bang."

"Your puns are awful," Thomas said. "I'm tired, and I have a big day tomorrow."

Blaze shook his head. "You're going to stand around, watching the movers pack, making sure they don't put a finger through the de Kooning or the Pollock. Other than that, you'll sit on the sofa working. So who cares?" He waited for Thomas's answer, and when he didn't have a good one, Thomas went into the bedroom to change.

"Why are you my friend again?" Thomas asked as he looked through his closet.

"That's easy. Because I'm the only person who won't let you sit around and wallow in your own crapulence on a Friday night." Blaze's voice drifted in from the other room. "Put on something hot, and make sure the pants are tight enough to show off your ass."

"Jesus, Blaze. I'm not twenty years old anymore. I don't need to do all that crap." Thomas grabbed a pair of comfortable jeans and tossed them on the bed, then went looking for a silk shirt he liked.

"We're damn near forty. We need to do all that crap and more. Have you looked in the mirror lately? Neither of us is fat, but we're spreading nonetheless. Our asses are wider and our legs thicker. We can't wear those skinny jeans we used to pour ourselves into when we were young. So now we have to show off the goods and remind the boys that with a little time comes a whole lot of experience."

Blaze always looked good, and Thomas had never noticed any spreading where his friend was concerned.

Thomas finished dressing and came out. "How is this, your highness?" He smirked.

"Good God. We're going out for the evening, to a club, not to a cotillion." Blaze brushed past him and went right to Thomas's closet. "Put this on, and those jeans look like you got them at Old Farts R Us." He dug through and tossed a pair of black jeans on the bed. "Put those on. Black is slimming."

"But that shirt is too small."

"Perfect. It should be tight to show off your arms." Blaze stepped out of the room, and Thomas wondered if this was worth it.

He changed clothes again. The jeans hugged his hips and waist so tightly that they were a second skin, and the shirt stretched over his chest. When he looked in the full-length mirror, he had to admit that he looked pretty good.

"All right. Let's go," Thomas said, emerging from the bedroom. Blaze nodded and turned toward the door. Thomas got his wallet and keys, followed Blaze out, and locked the apartment door. After taking the elevator down to the first floor, they were greeted by the doorman and then stepped out into the Upper West Side night air.

"I can't believe you're giving all this up," Blaze said as he hailed a cab. "What kind of place are you going to have in Colorado Springs?"

Thomas shrugged. "I don't know yet. I haven't bought a house. I figured I'd rent a place for a while and then move when I found somewhere I really liked." He wasn't dumb enough to buy anything sight unseen.

"You're moving pretty quickly with this whole thing." Blaze looked up and down the street, and they walked the block or so toward Fifth.

"Collin called a few weeks ago, and he said Mom and Dad were having a tougher time of it. They would never say anything, but mom's rheumatism is making it harder for her to get around, and Dad is having to do more and more for her. Collin helps, but he works strange hours at the restaurant, and, well...." Thomas shrugged. "I'm nearly forty and I'm tired." He stepped around a pile of dog leavings, wishing the offending owner had been given a huge ticket. "I've been working night and day to get this business started and then to make it successful. Now I want the chance to spend some time with my mom and dad before it's too late."

Blaze reached the corner, whistling shrilly for a cab. "The last thing I would ever think of is moving home to see my parents. God, I'd rather lose a leg than spend an hour back in Georgia with my father. The man is a fanatic. He turned his back on me as soon as he thought I might be gay." When a cab pulled to the curb, Blaze pulled open the back door to climb in, and Thomas got in as well. He should have called his limousine service and arranged a ride. That was, if Blaze had given him any kind of notice at all, like a normal person.

"The Brick," Blaze told the driver, who nodded, taking off.

"You really want to go there?" That gay club had been around for decades.

"It's been completely remodeled and is trendy again. Guys are done with that techno shit and want some good, clean… well, maybe more like hot and dirty action. This is the place where all the hot guys are right now." And Blaze would know. His gift was to keep up with what was gay, hot, and where his money could get him anything he wanted.

Thomas turned to Blaze. "Have you ever given any thought to settling down?"

Blaze's eyes burned in the semidarkness and flashing lights as the blocks passed. "Yeah, I did the whole relationship thing. Remember Mathias? He was…." Blaze seemed at a loss for words. "You know how well that all worked out." He shook his head. "I'm way better off without all those awful entanglements that only leave you wishing to hell that you hadn't let him in your heart… or your apartment." Blaze swore under his breath. "The bastard stole me blind, and I needed a course of penicillin to fully eradicate him. So, no, I haven't thought about settling down any time soon. I'll cruise the boys until I'm too ugly and old. And then just hire them."

Thomas knew the whole story about Mathias, but he hadn't fully realized how deeply the little shit had hurt Blaze. Which pissed Thomas off, because he should have been paying closer attention. He thought about trying to find Mathias just so he could teach the stupid piece of crap a lesson about messing with people. "You can't let one asshole dictate your outlook like that."

They pulled into Midtown, and Blaze turned toward the window. "Bullshit. I've been out with other guys, and things always end the same damn way." He didn't even look at Thomas as he spoke, but Thomas could hear the pain in his voice. "I have good friends that I can trust, and I go to clubs or bars when I want someone to warm my bed for a night." He finally shifted to look at Thomas again. "I always thought you felt the same way. I mean, you never dated anyone, not seriously."

"I never dated anyone... well, with the exception of Angus." Thomas rolled his eyes. The few times he had gone out with a guy more than once, something at work would come up and he'd end up cutting the date short or canceling. The guys got the message pretty quickly that his job came first and they were going to be a distant second. There were never any third dates—except for Angus, and that had turned into a total disaster... for both of them. "Not really."

"See, I figured you got hurt by some shithead and never told me."

"Nope. Just never had time." Thomas turned, looking out the window as the neighborhood changed from apartment buildings to clubs and businesses.

"Do you want a social life?" Blaze asked as the cab pulled over.

Thomas opened the door, thankful to be able to evade the question. He paid the driver and joined Blaze as the cab sped away from the curb.

"You didn't answer my question."

Thomas gazed at the line of guys waiting to get into the club. This was a bad idea. It was going to take hours for them to get inside, and the last thing he wanted to be doing was waiting in a fucking line on a Friday night. "I think I might. I don't know." He knew he was getting tired of spending his days at the office and his nights doing more work. "There has to be more to life than just this." He waved a hand in front of him, not really referring to the club, but things in general.

"No need to worry, my friend." Blaze walked up to the doorman, spoke to him for a few seconds, and then motioned. The velvet rope lifted out of their way, and they were inside, just like that.

Thomas didn't have time to think about it. Instantly he was surrounded by the throbbing beat of the music and the crush of men, many of them shirtless, ripped chests and bellies covered in a glistening sheen of sweat—beauty and sex on display everywhere he looked.

"Where do you want to start?" Blaze asked as a man sauntered right up to him. He was shorter—a pocket powerhouse, judging by all the muscles. He stood on his tiptoes and whispered something to Blaze before sliding his arm around Blaze's waist. Blaze smiled and made his way to the bar, while Thomas looked around once again, feeling like a junior high kid left standing by the wall while all the others danced.

Thomas, as the head of a very successful company built from the ground up, should be able to go out there and talk to guys. There wasn't anything to it. He talked to people all day long with no problem whatsoever. But right now, all the guys were gorgeous, tanned, toned... hot.

"Go on out there and meet people," Blaze said, pressing a beer glass into his hand before downing his shot and turning away with short-and-studly. They made their way to the dance floor, where Blaze smoothly took the other man in his arms and they burned it up. Even Thomas could see they were hot together, and he had been told on multiple occasions that he was pretty clueless about things like that. His own dance moves lay somewhere between a dying chicken and a scarecrow.

Thomas slowly approached the bar and found an empty place to watch what was happening. He finished his beer and ordered another one.

"Hey," said a man, about thirty, with jet-black hair and piercing eyes, as he leaned over the bar, glancing at Thomas.

"Hello," Thomas said, giving him his best smile. Why was he so nervous? Thomas quickly searched for something to say that didn't sound like a line. "Would you like a drink?"

"That would be nice, thanks." The guy settled next to him, smiling as Thomas got the bartender's attention and ordered a martini. "I've never been here before." He turned back to the dance floor, and Thomas followed his gaze. "I had no idea there would be so many older guys trolling for young dudes." The martini arrived, and then the guy was gone.

Thomas shook his head and paid for the drink. Being shot down before he even took a chance was one thing, but the guy being rude was dispiriting. If men were like that, Thomas didn't understand why anyone bothered at all.

He turned in his seat to watch as Blaze and Studly melded themselves together, dancing, or fucking standing up—it was hard to tell which. He ordered another drink and waited to see if there was anyone to try to talk with.

Thomas quickly realized this whole thing was a mistake. It only helped to drive the point home that he needed a change. Thomas threaded through the crowd to Blaze, explained that he was going home, and told him to have fun. Then he weaved out through the crush of bodies and into the night air. This time he called his car service, requested a limo, and waited, watching the boys in line. When the car pulled up, he got inside, ignoring the looks of curiosity, and rode home.

It was definitely time to get out of New York.

Chapter 2

BRANDON COULDN'T believe his grandmother had interfered... again.

"I didn't get you the job." She patted his cheek. "I only got you the address for where to send your résumé and stuff." She handed him the paper with the email address. "Grace Stepford said her son is coming back to town and will need to get an assistant. He's a bigwig from New York and really busy."

"I don't need to take an assistant job," he protested.

"You need to work, and he has plenty of contacts. So, if he likes you, that will be a boost up."

She had a point. He'd been looking for work for months, even before he graduated with his MBA, and he'd found nothing.

"I know." He hated to admit that she was right. Brandon sighed. "I'll go send it right now." He went into his room and opened his laptop. It didn't take him long to compose a nice email and attach his résumé. He was getting very good at this sort of thing.

"Bran," his grandma called right after he sent the message. "I have lunch ready."

He bounded out and sat at the table. His grandma was doing okay, but sometimes she needed some help. After graduating from Colorado State, he hadn't intended to return to Colorado Springs, but with the job situation the way it was right now, especially for new graduates, he didn't have a choice. "Which Stepford did I just apply to assist, exactly?" He probably should have asked before he sent the résumé.

"Thomas Stepford. Do you remember him? I think you used to mow his lawn before he left town and made it big." She set a plate with a sandwich on it in front of him and took the chair next to him at the old Formica-topped table. Nothing ever changed for his grandma. This table had been in this kitchen for as long as Brandon could remember. "He was always a very nice young man. Intense, though."

"I remember," Brandon said.

Boy, did he ever remember Thomas Stepford. Mr. Stepford, as he'd referred to him then, had started some sort of business and was really busy. Brandon had seen that he was home and screwed up his courage to go over and see if he wanted his lawn mowed. The grass was getting tall, and Brandon figured it wouldn't hurt to ask. He'd rung the bell and the door opened. Mr. Stepford was in just a pair of workout jeans, and Brandon remembered doing his best not to stare at the hotness in front of him.

Somehow he managed to get his little speech out and ask for the job. Mr. Stepford had smiled, which only made him hotter, and said he'd pay him twenty bucks a time to mow and edge the yard. He also said he'd pay him fifteen bucks an hour if he'd weed the front beds and trim the bushes. That was good money—like, really good money—and Brandon had quickly agreed and gotten to work once Mr. Stepford closed the door, cutting off the view that made Brandon salivate and provided late-night fantasy material for the rest of his teenage years.

Every time Brandon went to be paid, he hoped there would be a repeat of the view he'd gotten that first day, but no such luck. Well, once he'd walked over and found Mr. Stepford in the backyard, lying in a lawn chair, reading some papers. He was in a pair of shorts and a tank top that showed off his arms. But that was as close as he ever got to the view of heaven he'd received that first day.

"Brandon. Are you there?" his grandma teased, her voice pulling him out of his woolgathering.

"Yeah, sure." He took a bite of his sandwich. "I thought I'd take care of the yard this afternoon and do some cleaning up in the front." His grandma couldn't do that sort of thing anymore, and it needed to be done. Of course he'd help. She had been kind enough to let him stay with her so he wouldn't have to live with his mother and that jerk she'd married after the divorce. God, his mother had complained about his dad endlessly, but then married a jerk of epic proportions.

"I appreciate it." She patted his hand with her wrinkled one.

His grandparents had always been so easy to love. Their home had been a place of stability when his mom and dad were fighting, which they had done a lot, mostly about money. Which was totally ironic. Mom always thought that his dad was cheap. So in the end, she left him and married a man who pinched his pennies so hard, he could make Abe Lincoln scream.

"It's no problem." He finished his sandwich, took what was left of his iced tea out to the garage with him, and started the lawn mower.

He got the front and back yards mowed and began working on the front beds. They were pretty infested, but he got the weeds under control and trimmed the shrubs. After a good three hours' work, the front of the house looked much better. Brandon decided he'd buy some flowers to plant the next time he went out. Grandma loved flowers and they would make her happy.

Done for the day, he put everything away and went inside to clean up. He checked his email, and to his complete shock, found a response sent just half an hour earlier.

Mr. Wilson,

Thank you for your résumé. I'm Mr. Stepford's New York assistant, and we were impressed by your qualifications. Please call me at your earliest convenience so we can set up a time to speak with you.

Marjorie Westfield

She'd included a phone number, and Brandon debated whether he should call right away He didn't want to seem desperate, but he needed to get some sort of job so he could help out Grandma and stop sponging off her. He decided to take a shower, and once he was clean, he checked the time and made the call.

"Thomas Stepford's office," a cheerful but professional woman said as she answered the phone. "This is Marjorie."

He cleared his throat. "I'm Brandon Wilson, and I received your email and…."

"Oh, excellent," she said happily. "You are prompt. I like that. Your résumé was forwarded by HR because of your interest in being Mr. Stepford's assistant and because you're in Colorado Springs. Mr. Stepford is relocating there for the time being. He will need an assistant, and your résumé is quite impressive with your entrepreneurial efforts."

"What sort of duties will there be?" Brandon asked.

"He'll need you to run errands and work with me to maintain his calendar. I will keep his master calendar for him, but he'll need someone there to make sure he has what he needs. You'll be working directly with Mr. Stepford, but for me."

"I see," Brandon said.

"I doubt it." She chuckled. "I've been Mr. Stepford's assistant for ten years now, and he's a very busy man. He's hoping to be able to have more time with his parents, and to do that, he'll need someone who can assist him there. I'll take care of the corporate and business appointments, and you'll handle mostly personal errands and helping to make sure he stays on schedule."

She seemed nice enough from what he'd heard, and definitely businesslike. Which was very good. He could deal with professional people. "So I'll be sort of the assistant to the assistant?"

"No. More like his second assistant. You'll be working directly with him more than I will, but we'll need to coordinate things so everything runs smoothly and he isn't double-booked or run ragged." She paused. "Mr. Stepford has worked hard for many years to get where he is. That has also meant that he works long hours at a very fast pace. I believe he's hoping to be able to slow that pace when he's there. He deserves it if anyone does. It will be his assistant's job—our job, if things work out—to make sure that happens."

"I can definitely do that." Brandon smiled. "So what sort of questions do you have for me?"

They spent the next hour talking, and Brandon answered all the questions Marjorie fired at him. They spoke about his schooling, previous employment, and his hopes for the future. Then she asked where he saw himself in five years.

"Not as someone's assistant," Brandon answered, and realized that might be insulting to Marjorie, but she chuckled.

"Good answer. We all need to have bigger goals. You're just out of college. I'm sure you didn't get an MBA to be an assistant. If it were your life's ambition, I'd wonder." She seemed to have a great attitude, and Brandon thought he would like working with her, though he had to remind himself that he didn't have the job yet.

"When does Mr. Stepford need someone to start?"

"He will arrive in Colorado Springs tomorrow and is going to be visiting with his parents. His calendar is free until the following Monday, but I'd like you to meet him and get started earlier… say, Thursday. I'll get the paperwork started with HR, and they can have you fill out what they need. Then we can go from there."

"Sounds awesome." He grinned. It looked like Brandon had the job. It wasn't anything like he'd dreamed of once he had his masters, but it would mean some money coming in and he'd meet some people and maybe make some connections.

"I have your email address, as well as your phone number." Marjorie rattled it off. "Is that your cell?"

"Yes. You can reach me there anytime." He kept his voice level as they said their goodbyes, but once they ended the call, he let out a soft whoop and then went in search of his grandma.

He found her by the stove, putting a big pot on the burner. "I got the job! That was Mr. Stepford's assistant in New York, and she hired me to work with him here." That was a load off his mind.

"That's good." She patted him lightly on the back.

"I can work for him and keep looking for the job I really want." At least this would give him a chance to breathe, and he'd be working for Thomas Stepford, the hunk who still sometimes haunted his dreams. Of course, he'd have to be professional and couldn't go around gawking at his boss.

"When do you start?" Grandma asked as she pulled out ingredients.

"Thursday. They're going to send over all the papers I need to fill out." He told her all about the rest of the interview.

"I'm glad it all worked out." She continued stirring the pot on the stove. "I'm making sauce. They had good tomatoes at the market, and I want to get some made to put in the freezer. I can do this, so you might as well go out and have some fun. There's no need for you to sit around here with an old lady." She scooted him out of her kitchen with a smile.

Brandon went to his room. He could probably see if any of his friends were free, but instead he checked in online and ended up playing *Warlords of Garu* until it was time for dinner. After that, he helped Grandma with the dishes and cleaned up around the house until it was time to go to bed.

He lay quietly, staring up at the ceiling, wondering what Mr. Stepford looked like now. He closed his eyes, and the image he'd called up many times of Thomas in only his pants flashed in his mind's eye. Brandon took a deep breath, wiping that image away. He would be working for Thomas, and that meant he needed to be professional at all times. Brandon was not going to be perving on his boss, because that was just too stereotypical for words. Not only that, but he had no idea if Mr. Stepford was gay and… heck, he was Mr. Stepford. He was, well, older than him.

Brandon released the breath he'd been holding. This was a job, and he would do it to the very best of his ability.

"BRANDON… IS it okay if I call you Brandon?" Marjorie asked when she called a few days later while he was outside working in Grandma's yard.

"Of course," he said brightly, wiping his forehead and no doubt smearing dirt all over his sweaty skin.

"Good. We got all your information. Once again, thank you for being prompt." He heard a smile in her voice. "You have no idea how pleased I am to be working with you."

"I'm glad to be working with you too. But I have one question. We never talked about my salary or what my work hours would be. There was nothing in the information sent about any of that. I was wondering…."

"Of course. Like I said, we got all your paperwork, but there's one more step before I can hire you. Mr. Stepford is the one to make the final decision. I went ahead with the paperwork because I think he's going to be very pleased with you. I called to set up a time so he can meet you." Clicking sounded in the background. "I know this is unusual, but I needed to get things moving. Let me see. Mr. Stepford is at his parents' for a few days until his rental is cleaned, and he has said he'll be free this afternoon after two. I'll email you the address. Can you be there at two thirty? Will that work?"

"Yes. I'll be there then." His phone vibrated, and a message popped up at the top of the screen. "I just got your email."

"Wonderful. Once I have his approval, I'll send you a company phone and iPad, along with access to his calendar and other files you'll need."

Brandon cleared his throat. "Will he want me to drive him places?"

"I doubt it. He has said he'll drive himself. But you do have a car to run errands and things, right? Keep track of miles, and we will reimburse you for mileage." She sounded a little scattered, and Brandon wondered at it, but he didn't know her well enough to understand why. "Once you've met with him, I'll go over all other details."

"No problem." Brandon smiled.

Marjorie said she'd speak to him after he met with Mr. Stepford, then ended the call.

Brandon hurried to the bathroom and started the shower. He jumped in to clean up and then dressed in nice clothes. He wasn't sure how he should look when interviewing for an assistant's job. He thought business casual was probably good. A suit was most likely overboard.

Still, he put on a nice pair of slacks, a light blue short-sleeve, button-down shirt, and nice shoes that weren't sneakers, and made sure his hair looked good. And he'd shaved again, so there was no scruff. He left his room, following the scent of cookies to the kitchen. A plate covered in plastic wrap rested on the edge of the counter.

"What are those for?"

"Take them with you. Grace has a real sweet tooth, and she's had a hard time of it lately." Grandma handed him the plate, and Brandon took it, wondering how it was going to look for him to be taking some of her cookies to a job interview. Still, he kissed her on the cheek, left the house, and drove to the address Marjorie had emailed to him.

Brandon parked on the street in front of the house and walked up to the door, carrying the cookies his grandma had sent. He knocked softly, then stepped back and waited. Dogs barked inside the house, and he instantly tensed. Brandon was allergic to all animals, especially dogs and cats, and he could already feel his nose begin to tingle in anticipation. If he'd known, he'd have taken some of his allergy medication.

The door opened and the yapping grew louder as two Lhasa apsos jumped at the bottom of the screen door. Brandon lifted his gaze to where Thomas Stepford stood in the doorway. "I'm Brandon Wilson.

Marjorie asked me to come by and talk with you about being your assistant here in town."

"Yes," Thomas said gruffly and, after telling the dogs to get back, pushed the door open. "She told me she had arranged for someone to come over."

Brandon stepped inside and his eyes watered. He blinked to try to keep his reaction at bay, but it didn't do very much. The house had been closed up because of the air-conditioning, and the dog dander had had a chance to really build up. All Brandon could hope for was that he wasn't inside too long and could get out before his reaction became too severe and he was reduced to a sneezing mess.

Mr. Stepford closed the door. "What's this?" he asked, looking at the plate Brandon was carrying.

"My grandmother sent these over for your mom." He was about to hand the plate to Mr. Stepford when he sneezed loudly.

The dogs yipped and the plate went flying out of his hands. Brandon groaned as the plastic wrap gave way and cookies flew in every direction. The plate shattered on the floor, and bits of cookie ended up everywhere.

What a way to make a first impression.

Brandon wanted to crawl under the sofa and hide, but that would only send his allergies into overdrive.

"Buddy, Clementine, go in the other room." They ignored him, and Mr. Stepford scooped both dogs into his arms and went out back to let them outside.

Brandon sneezed again and wondered how he could clean up the mess he'd made.

"Look, I'm sorry." He could feel the job he'd thought he had slipping out of his grasp. "Let me help clean this up." He sneezed again, the sound echoing through the house.

"It's all right. Give me a minute." Mr. Stepford got a trash can and threw everything, including the pieces of the plate, in it. Then he got out the vacuum, which only seemed to add more dust to the air. Brandon left the room and sat at the kitchen table until Mr. Stepford was done. "Okay. I'm going to guess that you're allergic."

Brandon nodded. He turned to where two small doggie faces peered in the sliding glass doors. "Sorry. I didn't know or I'd have taken some medication." The stuff made him sleepy as hell and dried him out to the point that he felt like a desert, but it got him through when he needed it.

"How about we go outside?" Mr. Stepford said.

Brandon couldn't get out of the house fast enough.

Mr. Stepford let the dogs back in, and they left the house. Brandon took as deep a breath as he could, sneezing a few more times as his eyes began to clear. He knew it would take a while for the rest of his symptoms to dissipate.

"Marjorie said you would be over."

"She told me that you wanted to meet me and that you'd go over the kinds of things you thought I'd be doing for you." Thankfully they stopped on the sidewalk out in front of the house. This was a strange place to conduct an interview, but Brandon was grateful he could breathe once again. "I graduated with an MBA a few months ago. I'm a hard worker, and I know I can do whatever you need me to do."

Brandon took a good look at Mr. Stepford and had to admit he was even more attractive now. The years had been generous to him. There was the slightest hint of gray at the temples of his otherwise jet-black hair, and his eyes were as piercing as they had been. He was broader and seemed stronger, more solid, and definitely as hot as the Mr. Stepford he remembered.

"An MBA, that's very good," Mr. Stepford said. "But if you have that kind of degree, why do you want to be my assistant?" His deep brown eyes stared intensely at Brandon, who forced his mind to stay on track.

"Well... shoot...," he demurred, then figured honesty was best. "I need a job. I got my degree and I did very well in school. Marjorie has all the details and that. Right now, I'm living with my grandmother, and I can't keep sponging off her. She and your mom are friends, and I got the word that you needed some help, so I applied."

"I see," Mr. Stepford said skeptically.

Brandon knew he only had once chance to try to salvage this entire situation. "I had one job all through high school, and then when I left, I spent all four years of undergrad waiting tables. I work hard and I don't change jobs on a whim. Learning the business world from the ground up is important, regardless of the title. If you want someone who will do their best to be a good assistant, then that's me." He shifted his weight from foot to foot, meeting Mr. Stepford's gaze with his own until he was wracked by a sneeze and wanted to crawl into a hole somewhere. "Thank you for meeting with me." Not extending his hand because he had just sneezed all over it, he went back to his car, knowing he'd blown that interview so sky-high, it was pathetic.

Chapter 3

"HE WHAT?" Marjorie asked when Thomas described what had happened.

"Yeah. Sneezed all over everything through the entire interview." Thomas chuckled.

Marjorie clicked her tongue. "And you didn't do anything to help him." Man, she sounded pissed. "The poor man had an allergic reaction to your mom's dogs and you think that's funny." No, she was way beyond angry and well into livid. "I'd probably be as miserable as he was, but I'd have said something."

He knew she would have too.

"You need an assistant there. I can manage your schedule and calendar for you, but I can't get your cleaning and run the errands that always seem to come up at the last damn minute." Marjorie really had a head of steam, and Thomas wondered who was the boss. "That young man has an impressive résumé, and

I liked him when we talked on the phone. He's funny, and he doesn't have an agenda like the others I talked to did."

"Others?" Thomas asked as he absently searched through some papers.

"Yes. I talked to eight candidates. One was clearly more interested in you being single than she was in the job. Two of them chewed gum, cracking it like teenagers through the entire phone interview. I wanted to box their ears. I swear one of them didn't have the brains God gave a rock, and the others were completely unsuitable and set off more alarm bells than a prison breakout. Brandon was nice, respectful, and he's interested... until you sabotaged him with your mother's walking balls of barking death."

"Okay. I think that's enough." He didn't snap, but he was firm. Something seemed to have gotten into Marjorie.

"You need someone to help you out there. Just because you're out of New York doesn't mean you're going to sit around with your feet up. I know you. You're going to work and get caught up in some deal. Then you'll forget to have your laundry done, and, hell, you'll realize one night that you're starving and there's nothing in the house to eat, and I won't be there."

"I'm not that bad," he protested. "I'm an adult and can take care of myself."

"Really? You do realize that groceries come from a store? They don't magically appear in your refrigerator. The same with plumbers and repairmen. Someone has to call them and be there when they arrive. You never saw any of that. Just like your clothes. They aren't

washed by elves and magically reappear back where
they belong. I took care of that for years. Well, me and
Darlene. She did most of the running when I had to be
at the office. But it got done because your assistants
made sure you could be as productive as possible."

"Darlene? Who's Darlene?" Thomas didn't recall
ever hearing that name before.

Marjorie sighed. "Your housekeeper. She did
your household running and cleaned up while you
were gone. I engaged her years ago. She's a wonderful
lady, and you never met her because you didn't need
to. We took care of what needed to be done. And so
you know, Darlene is retiring and going to live with
her daughter upstate. You gave her a nice bonus and
sent a card."

"To someone I never met…. How did I miss
that?" he asked quietly. Thomas knew Marjorie handled a lot of things for him so he could concentrate on
what was important. He didn't realize just how far into
his work he'd fallen.

"Because I took care of it. And you asked to meet
your assistant in Colorado Springs, and I let you. But
that young man is the only one who seemed a likely
prospect for the job. Are you really going to discount
him because he's allergic to dogs?"

Thomas groaned. "I suppose not."

"Then good," Marjorie chirped. "How much are
you going to offer him? You need to give some thought
to the kind of things you're going to want him to do
for you. If you give your okay, I'll handle everything
on this end and have him report for duty on Thursday.
That's when you should be able to get into your rented
house. He can help with the movers."

He heard her clicking away, knowing she was doing her usual multitasking thing. "All right. I'll trust you on this one." She was the one person who never let him down.

"Good. I'll call him tomorrow, settle the details with him, and tell him when and where to show up. I'm texting you his phone number for now. I'll be sending him some company equipment so he can get started."

"Fine," Thomas agreed.

"Okay. Why all this resistance? He couldn't have been that bad. On the phone he had energy and seemed eager."

Thomas could almost see Marjorie's perfectly plucked eyebrows rise. "He was."

"Then what's the problem?" she pressed.

Leave it to Marjorie to call him on his bullshit. Almost everyone else was too enthralled and nodded their damned heads at him.

"He's...." Thomas gulped. "You never saw him, did you?"

"What, is he ugly or something?" she teased, then chuckled. "I looked him up on the internet and thought he was rather cute-looking. And from his Facebook account, I'd say he was gay, though it doesn't state that explicitly." Marjorie paused, and he heard her gasp. "I take it he's really cute and he floats your boat." Then she started laughing.

"It's not funny. He's so much younger than I am, and I'm not going to get involved with my assistant. God, that's so tacky. Not to mention stupid. I mean, really."

Marjorie continued chuckling. "Just think. The great Thomas Stepford being attracted to his assistant. I have to ask, do you think you can behave professionally with this boy? Because if not, I will have to try to find someone else." She grew quiet for ten seconds, then laughed again.

"I don't see what's so funny." He waited while her laughter died away.

"You. I have known you for twelve years and worked for you for most of them. Other than once—and we both know what kind of mistake Angus was—you have never shown any interest in anyone. There have been men in this office who have flirted with you nonstop... gorgeous men, and you never noticed any of them. So yeah... I think you'll treat Brandon professionally and with respect."

"You really are a pain in the ass sometimes," Thomas groused and sighed.

"Is that Marjorie?" his mother said as she came into the room, followed by both of the dogs. Buddy jumped up into Thomas's lap and made himself comfortable.

"Yes. Do you want to talk to her? She's only giving me grief right now about my new assistant." He held out the phone, and his mother shook her head.

"Just tell her I said hello." She sat down. "Oh, is it Thelma's grandson?" she asked as she lifted her knitting bag and slowly got to work. With her rheumatism, she couldn't work as fast as she used to, but it was good therapy for her and helped keep her joints limber.

"Yes. Marjorie thinks I have a thing for him and is wondering if I can keep professional." He rolled his eyes, and his mother looked up at him with a shrug.

"You better be professional. He used to mow your lawn when he was a kid."

Thomas nearly dropped the phone. He'd been trying to figure out why Brandon looked familiar, and now the pieces fell into place.

"Marjorie, I need to go." He felt himself paling, and he didn't want to listen to her laughter when she found out about this. "Just take care of things."

"Of course."

Thomas put his phone in his pocket. "What are you talking about?" he asked his mom. "He used to what?"

"Brandon Wilson was the young man who mowed your lawn when you were still living here. Remember? He took that tangle of a lawn you had and made it nice. That was before the business really took off and you decided to move everything to New York."

"How old was he then?" Thomas asked a little breathlessly.

"About fifteen, I'd think. Why?"

Thomas shivered as he tried to remember. Brandon had been tall even then, lanky and handsome, with the best eyes. Not that Thomas spent a great deal of time watching him. He'd been aware that he was a kid, and there had been no way he was going to perv on someone underage.

"No reason." That would make the adult Brandon about twenty-five, and man, he'd grown up handsome. That was for sure. "Marjorie is handling the last of the employment stuff for him."

His mom smiled. "That's very nice of you. That's going to help both of them a lot." She continued her knitting, so Thomas put the dog on the floor, stood, and wandered through the house he'd grown up in to the backyard.

As soon as the door slid open, both dogs raced over and filed outside, turning around to see where he was going.

"You're little pests," he said with no heat. They were largely good dogs, and when he sat on the lounger in the shade, they both jumped up and settled around him.

He'd come here to try to simplify his life, maybe even enjoy some free time and relax. What he hadn't expected were complications, like an assistant who was drop-dead gorgeous and made his heart race a little faster. He'd always hired women to avoid any sort of attraction when he needed someone close to him. That was how he'd found Marjorie, and Karen before her.

Thomas groaned and lay back, closing his eyes. The dogs snuggled closer, as if knowing he had a dilemma to contend with. Not that it really mattered. None of it did. Brandon was going to be his assistant, and that meant he could treat him the same way he did Marjorie and everyone else who worked for him. It didn't matter that Brandon was walking, talking sex appeal, or that he had the bluest eyes and the longest lashes Thomas had ever seen. None of that was important. He had to ignore it, as well as the way his heart raced just by having Brandon standing close to him. He'd tell himself that a million times if he had to. None of that mattered. Brandon was going to work for him and that was all that counted. He'd been down the road of dating an employee and it had been a disaster. He wasn't doing it again.

THOMAS SPENT the rest of the day and the next doing very little, like he was on vacation. Not that he took regular vacations, but he felt good and his calendar was largely free. Marjorie only sent him a single text to let him know that Brandon had accepted the job as his assistant and that he would be at the house he'd rented Thursday morning to meet the movers and help oversee that things were properly unloaded. Apparently Marjorie had also hired people who would unpack everything and a decorator to set up the house. Thomas could move things around, of course, but the initial unpacking would be done.

Thursday morning, Thomas got up, dressed, and drove over to his home early in the morning. Marjorie had helped him find the house. It was bigger than he'd set out to get, but it was available, so he'd taken it. Renting left his options open. The plan was for him to live here for six months or so until he got settled in the area and knew what he wanted. Then he could decide if he liked it here and wanted to settle down or if he would go back to New York.

There was a car already in the circular drive, so he parked behind it. He went inside and found Brandon standing in the entrance hall.

"Good morning, Mr. Stepford," Brandon said as he entered. "Your mother forwarded a key via my grandmother. I hope it's okay that I got started."

"Thomas, please," he said without thinking as he looked around. He'd seen pictures of the house, but this was the first time he'd been inside.

"All right. Thomas." Brandon smiled, and Thomas's heart beat a little faster. He pushed away the zip of attraction and kept his mind on the task at hand. "Marjorie apparently sent a list of your furniture and things to a designer, and they developed some basic plans for placement. She sent that over to me yesterday, and I've been reviewing it."

"What do you think?"

"After seeing the house, I think she had some good ideas, but other things are going to be problematic. We can make adjustments as we go." Brandon seemed excited, and Thomas watched as he left the entryway, heading to the large living room. "She has the television in here, but I thought it would be better in the room in the back off the kitchen. It's cozier and less formal."

"All right. You do what you think is best," Thomas said as he turned to leave the room.

Brandon stared after him.

"What is it?"

"Don't you care? This is going to be your home. Maybe for just as long as you rent it, but you're going to live here. Don't you care where things get put?" Brandon scratched his head.

Thomas shrugged. "It's only for a few months. So what does it really matter?" His phone rang and Thomas pulled it out of his pocket. "Hey, Blaze."

"Do you miss New York yet?"

Thomas chuckled. "Not really. The movers are about to arrive at the house I rented. Though I don't know what I'm going to do with all this space." He turned to look through the large rooms. "I have a small dining table. The room here could fit a table for twelve."

"No shit?" Blaze asked. "Damn, I forget sometimes that the rest of the world doesn't live in tiny apartments and raise a family of four in eleven hundred square feet. I suppose you're not going to know what to do with it all."

"I'll figure it out." He turned, watching as Brandon reviewed the furniture layouts, occasionally glancing his way and then back to what he was doing. "How are you? How are things there?"

"No different. I mean, you haven't been gone all that long, and everything is just fine. The Swanson deal is moving forward without a hitch, and the Hell's Kitchen building just received the final approvals, so construction is getting ready to start. Everything is sailing along."

"Good." Thomas sighed softly and let go of some of the trepidation he'd had about moving away. "I'm glad."

"No, you're not," Blaze said. "You'd be happier if everything had fallen apart in your absence and you had to come back and save the day." He laughed. "Don't give me any of your crap. I know you too well. You live for this place."

Thomas stifled a groan. "I used to." He tried to keep the disappointment from his voice, but he probably failed.

"What's with the sadness? Is there something you haven't told me?"

Leave it to Blaze to become insightful all of a sudden.

"Maybe." Thomas turned to where Brandon had opened the front door to let the movers inside. He led them through the hall and out of Thomas's sight. "It's nothing serious. Just that the doctors told me I needed a break from all the stress. They are worried about my blood pressure and the fact that things… are…." He didn't want to talk about this. The doctors had been worried about his digestive issues and stomach pains.

"Then you best take care of yourself. We have things in hand here. Maybe in a few weeks, once the Swanson deal is finalized, I'll fly out to see you."

"I think I'd like that." Thomas smiled as he thought of seeing his best friend once again.

"Good. Now take it easy and, damn you, I wish you'd said something before." Blaze sounded more than a little pissed.

"It's no big deal. Mom and Dad needed me here, and I needed a break and to take things slower. It seemed like this was the right thing to do for now. I can try to let go of some of the stress and see what Mom and Dad need." He shrugged as the movers began carrying in boxes. Brandon stood at the door like an adorable traffic cop, pointing and laughing with the guys as they passed.

"Thomas, are you there?" Blaze asked. "Are you listening to me?"

"Sorry. My attention was pulled elsewhere." *Yeah, exactly where it doesn't need to be. You don't need to be watching Brandon every chance you get.*

"I can tell. You get done what you need to and call me when you have a chance, okay? We can talk some more." Blaze ended the call, and Thomas put the phone in his pocket, then joined Brandon at the door.

"Is everything under control?"

Brandon turned to look at him, and their gazes met for just a few seconds, but a shiver went up Thomas's spine, and he swallowed, taking a step back. But the intensity that passed between them didn't dissipate.

"Yes." Brandon turned away and cleared his throat. "There's a large team of movers." He stepped back as boxes were brought in and distributed through the house. "That goes in the room next to the kitchen instead of the living room," Brandon directed the movers.

As he returned to his post, his scent reached Thomas's nose, clean and masculine, with just a hint of cologne that only added to the male intensity that washed off him. Thomas had to stop himself from inhaling deeply.

"There are two large wooden cases on the truck. Have them put in the living room and don't have them opened. They can stay that way for now." He'd figure out where he wanted to put them and then have them professionally hung.

"All right." Brandon made a note and stepped back as the movers brought in the sofa. He excused himself and followed them, directing them on the placement, then returned. Brandon seemed efficient and careful, which was a plus. But every time he turned to Thomas, with those eyes.... Thomas had seen that color once, when he was in the Caribbean. The blue of the sea when the sun shone on it. The color was stunning, and Thomas could watch it all day.

"I need to make some calls," he said, and left the room just to get away from Brandon. Man oh man, he was in deep trouble. His willpower was draining away after only an hour with Brandon. He needed to get it together and put this crap aside. Brandon worked for him, and that meant he was off-limits.

Besides, what would a handsome young guy like him see in an old man about to turn forty?

Chapter 4

BRANDON KNEW instinctively where Thomas was in the house. His job was to try to anticipate what Thomas was going to need, so he kept an eye on him, which wasn't hard at all. Thomas was more than easy on the eyes, and Brandon was drawn to him just like he had been when he'd mowed his lawn all those years ago. Not that he was going to do anything about it. Attraction or not, he was going to be professional.

"Thomas," Brandon said as gently as he could when he found his boss lying on the back-porch chaise, one of the few pieces of furniture left at the house by the previous occupants. Thomas's eyes were closed, and he actually looked relaxed, at ease… and stunning. The lines around his eyebrows and mouth had smoothed out, and his hair was slightly askew. His chest rose and fell at regular intervals, and his jeans hugged his thighs invitingly. He was handsome, to say the least. Brandon hated to disturb him, but he had some questions. When Thomas didn't stir, he touched his shoulder, and Thomas opened his eyes. "Sorry."

Thomas sat up, wiping his face. "Nothing to be sorry for." He blinked a few times, looking around, probably trying to get his bearings.

"There are a number of questions about the master bedroom. There are three large rooms in this place, and they all have attached bathrooms. Which one do you want?" Brandon felt like a fool.

"Doesn't matter," Thomas grumbled.

"Are you sure?" Brandon asked.

Thomas got up with a huff, and Brandon followed him, doing his best not to watch as he climbed the stairs after him. It was hard—pun intended, because he was getting there himself, watching Thomas's butt encased in those jeans.

At the top of the steps, Brandon pointed at one of the rooms. "This is the master, but it's in the front of the house." He opened the other door. "This room is just as big. The only difference is the closet. But it's in the back and would be quieter. So will that one." He indicated the third room. "Do you have a preference?"

Thomas looked at both rooms. "It really doesn't matter after all those years in New York. It's never quiet there. But put me in the room in the back." He pulled open the closet door. "This will be just fine."

"Okay. What size is your bed?" Brandon asked, and Thomas turned to him, their eyes meeting once more.

"King," he answered in a gruff tone.

Brandon swallowed and nodded, his imagination taking a short flight of erotic fantasy, wondering what

Thomas would look like on a deep green king-size duvet. After two seconds, he shook his head slightly and tapped his face with his hand to pull himself back to reality. "Then we can put the bed on this wall and the dresser over here. There's a chest on the plan for one of the guest rooms, so we could put that at the end of your bed if you like."

"Sure." Thomas smiled slightly and patted Brandon's shoulder, sending a wave of heat through him. It was an innocent touch, and Brandon pushed his reaction away. He was overreacting, which needed to end.

"I'll have the movers bring the things up. Have you given any thought to where you want the pictures to go? Oh, and those two large crates are downstairs. They look like they made it through in good condition."

"Thank you. Umm, just leave the pictures for now, I guess."

Thomas looked like he could use that nap Brandon had interrupted, so Brandon shooed him out, then directed the movers up the stairs with the bed. Once they had the bed and mattress placed, he dug through the boxes for the bedding and pillows and made up the bed for him. Then he shut the door and headed downstairs again.

The truck was nearly empty, with the last of the furniture being placed. The rooms were spare, but that wasn't anything he could help. The kitchen and family area seemed comfortable enough. One of the movers had organized the kitchen, and the rest were either bringing in the last of the things or taking out empty boxes and wrappings.

"Thomas," Brandon said when he found him once again on the back porch. "I went ahead and set up your bedroom for you." The bags under his eyes told him Thomas hadn't been sleeping. "I can handle the rest of this for you if you need some time alone." He wasn't going to suggest sleep, though it seemed to be what Thomas needed.

"Thanks." Thomas's phone rang as Brandon went back to supervising the last of the move. If Thomas wasn't going to take a few minutes to rest when he obviously needed it, there was little Brandon could do except try to help him as much as possible.

An hour later, the movers were packing up the last of their boxes and furniture pads. The living room had only a few pieces of furniture in it because most of the pieces had been diverted into the family area so Thomas could relax when he wanted to. Brandon figured Thomas could buy whatever he wanted for the other room. His goal had been to make Thomas as comfortable as possible.

He was making a final pass through the house when Marjorie called.

"How is the move going?"

"Excellent. Most things are unpacked, and I set up Thomas's room for him and got his clothes hung in his closet. I figured he could put away the things in his dresser. The decorator did a pretty poor job with colors and such, so I ended up moving a lot of things around. Thomas seemed to like what I did, though."

"Then that's what counts," Marjorie said. "Is he getting any rest at all?"

Brandon rolled his eyes. "He was lying down for a little this afternoon, but he's been on the phone for most of the day. I think someone is calling him every ten minutes or so. He's on the phone now." Brandon bit his lower lip to keep from telling Marjorie how he thought Thomas looked. Thomas was a grown man and didn't need him tattling on him.

"I'll see what I can do."

"But he's the boss. Wouldn't he just tell people not to call if he didn't want them too?" Brandon asked.

Marjorie sighed. "No. Thomas is a very good man and a great boss. He'd never tell anyone not to call. Instead he tries to solve their issues, and everyone in this damn place calls him instead of trying to solve problems they can do themselves with a little thought." Man, she sounded aggravated. "I'll talk to a few people here, see if they can't help."

"Okay." He really didn't feel it was something he should get involved with. "Is there anything else I need to do today?"

"No. I sent you a phone and iPad that you can use, and I'll email you the log-in information so you can access his calendar." She typed in the background, and then a phone rang. Marjorie put him on hold to take the other call.

He held the door as the last of the movers left the house. One of the men returned with a paper for him to sign. Brandon looked it over, signed for the delivery, and then closed the door after them. The house was quiet, and Brandon went into the sparse living room while he waited for Marjorie.

"Sorry," she said when she returned, still typing. "No. You should check with Thomas and then go on home. If you got him settled in his house, then you did your job for the day."

"Thanks, Marjorie."

"That's a big job." She seemed pleased, which made Brandon happy. "I'll talk to you tomorrow unless something comes up." She said goodbye and hung up.

Brandon put his phone back in his pocket and went to find Thomas. He found him in the kitchen. The dishes had been put away, but there were no groceries and the refrigerator was empty. Thomas was just closing the door as he came in.

"Can you run to the store?"

Brandon nodded. "What do you want me to get?" He prepared to take notes, but Thomas looked at him as though he had two heads. "I can't read your mind."

"Marjorie always takes care of it and…." Thomas paused as though he was surprised. "I never paid that much attention to what was in the house. I either ate what was there or went out and got something from around the corner."

"I can have some food delivered. Do you want pizza? I think one of the Chinese places will deliver." Brandon pulled out his phone and ran a search for takeout in the area. "If you put together a list, I can pick things up for you. What would you like?"

"Sushi," Thomas offered.

"All right." Brandon found a place and brought up the menu. "Let me know what you want, and I'll call in the order and get it." Thomas dictated his order, and Brandon called it in, adding something for himself. "I'll be right back."

He drove to the small strip center a few miles away and waited while they finished filling the order. In the meantime he messaged Marjorie about what Thomas liked to drink, and after getting the sushi, stopped at Starbucks for a latte and a macchiato and hurried back to the house.

"Thomas, I got your lunch," he called as he came back in, heading toward the kitchen. It seemed strange to just walk into someone else's house. He found Thomas watching ESPN in the open family room and handed him his coffee. Apparently the rental had come with the cable connected. Brandon made a mental note to check with Marjorie about it.

"You're a lifesaver," Thomas said, reaching for the coffee.

Brandon brought his sushi on a plate and set it on the coffee table. Then he went into the kitchen and pulled a stool up to the counter.

"What are you doing?" Thomas asked as he turned to him.

"I didn't want to bother you," Brandon said.

"Please join me if you like." Thomas rolled his eyes.

Brandon picked up his coffee and the package of sushi, brought it in, and sat in a chair. He carefully put his lunch on the coffee table. "Thanks." He took a bite of California roll and sipped his drink after he swallowed. "Are you pleased with how things are?"

"Yes." Thomas ate and watched the tennis match on television. "You did a good job. Thank you." He didn't look away from the screen, so Brandon ate and let Thomas do what he wanted. This was his house, after all, but if he didn't want to eat alone, then why ignore him once Brandon had sat down? It seemed kind of rude to him.

The match continued, and Brandon finished eating, then threw away the trash. Once Thomas was done, he took care of his dishes and left him to watch his match. He called Marjorie and got a list of groceries, then made a quick run to the store so Thomas didn't starve.

"If there's nothing else, I'll go on home. You have my number, so call if you need anything."

Thomas's phone rang and he answered it, nodding and waving to him. Brandon figured he was being dismissed and left the room. He closed the door before heading out to his car for the drive back to his grandma's house. It looked like he'd made it through his first day without embarrassing himself.

"How was your first day at work?" Grandma asked from where she stood at the stove when he got home.

Brandon inhaled, smiling at the scent of his grandma's chili. It was a perennial favorite. "Good. Though I didn't imagine I'd be using my MBA to manage someone's move into their rental house." It wasn't how he pictured his first job at all.

Grandma tapped her spoon on the side of the pot and set it on the holder. "But did you help him?"

Brandon nodded. "Yeah, I think so. I got his house set up, picked up some lunch, and got groceries for him. But then the calls started and he had that phone to his ear the rest of the day." It was too bad. Thomas should be able to have a moment's peace. Brandon pulled out one of the old kitchen chairs and sat down. His grandma put a plate with a couple of cookies on it in front of him, and he felt a wave of guilt. He hadn't told her about the sneezing fit at the interview or the cookie casualties. If she asked, he'd say the plate got broken and leave it at that.

"Then you need to do what you can to be there for him. That's what he hired you for." Grandma sat down as well, sighing softly.

"You're trying to do too much," Brandon said gently. He'd been worried that she never seemed to stop and that she was looking as tired as Thomas.

"I'm fine. I cook and bake. It isn't like I'm a stevedore." She patted his hand, and Brandon got up and made some decaf. It was what his grandma drank. Brandon thought the stuff tasted pretty vile, but he supposed if it was all he drank, he'd probably get used to it if he had nothing else to compare it to. "What are you doing tomorrow?"

Brandon set a mug of coffee in front of her. "Don't know. I'm still feeling my way around. I'll go on over in the morning and see what he needs. Marjorie will probably have stuff for me to do." Brandon picked up a cookie. "I'll probably need to find someone to be the housekeeper for him." He set down the cookie and wondered what Thomas liked to eat. Thomas had pretty much wolfed down the sushi. "I need to arrange some meals for Thomas."

"Talk to him and see if he'll open up a little. I bet he'll tell you the kind of thing he likes."

Brandon nodded. "Do you remember him from before he went away? I mowed his yard, but I don't know much else. He was always busy even back then."

"He was an energetic one, that's for sure. Always working and scraping. His mom and dad didn't have much. After Thomas was old enough to be in school, Grace went to work in the office at the Crawford's

Department Store downtown until they closed. His dad worked at the mill outside town. They had the best life they could afford, but Grace always told me that she felt like she wasn't doing enough for Thomas. That he always seemed to want more."

"I guess I can see that. He didn't get to be a big success without having his eye on what he wanted." Brandon had seen that in many of the case studies in school. People who were driven by some sort of internal need often succeeded.

"He mowed lawns probably starting when he was twelve and did a good job, the same way you did." She smiled at him. "Grace told me once that he was working too hard and had more work than he could do." Grandma sipped from her mug. "I remember Thomas out working until the sun set some nights. Then he hired another kid to work for him. Thomas had some sort of arrangement." She shook her head. "It wasn't long before Thomas had a business and he was mowing most of the lawns in the area, with two or three boys working for him."

"Wow." Brandon was impressed.

"That lasted until Thomas went to college, I guess. I don't know what he did when he was at school, but Grace said Thomas started a business there to help support himself." Grandma shrugged. "After that, there was no turning back for him. He bought a house here a few years after college and was working in real estate, and then sold it when he moved to New York. I was surprised that he left the area, because of Grace and Harold, but he was always driven to want more than what we had here." She patted the table softly, like that part of the conversation was over.

Brandon told himself that his curiosity about Thomas, his wanting to know what made him tick, was so he could do his job better, but really he was a little nosey. Thomas fascinated him. "Are you glad he's back?"

She tapped the table nervously. "Grace is, and I'm happy for her."

Brandon noticed her lack of a smile and the doubt in her eyes.

"I think… I don't know. It will hurt Grace and Harold pretty badly if Thomas doesn't like it here and moves away once again. They were so happy when he told them he was coming." She finished her coffee and stood to return to the stove to stir her pot. "All you can do is your best."

"I know, Grandma," Brandon said, finishing his cookies and putting his dishes in the dishwasher.

He went to his room and logged on to his computer to check his email. Before he'd gotten the job with Thomas, he'd sent out so many résumés and job enquiries, it was probably pathetic. He'd trolled Monster and other job sites for days, trying to find leads. At least he had some money coming in, and he was even being paid pretty well.

His phone rang, and he snatched it up. "Yes, Thomas," he said when he saw his number. "What do you need?"

"I have a list of items for you to get at the store…," Thomas said, and Brandon made a note in his to-do list. "Could you go first thing in the morning?"

"Of course. I'm assuming that you have laundry and things to be taken care of… and I wanted to ask, do you want me to help engage a housekeeper?"

"That would be great." Thomas sighed. "I have another call…. I'll see you in the morning." The call ended and Brandon stared at the phone.

What the hell was that? There had been nothing in that call that Thomas couldn't have waited until tomorrow morning to tell him. Maybe Thomas had been thinking of it and decided to call so he didn't forget? After all, he was still getting those calls.

HIS GRANDMA'S chili was amazing as usual, and Brandon was stuffed and a little bored. He thought of watching television, but that would mean sitting with his grandma while she watched her shows. Granted, hers weren't bad or anything, but if he had to watch another rerun of *The Big Bang Theory*, his head was going to explode. Especially those early seasons that he'd seen eighteen times.

His phone vibrated in his room, and he hurried to get it in case it was Thomas again. The screen flashed George Hansen. Brandon grinned and answered the call. "George," he said brightly, "what's up?"

"Nothing. Just sitting here trying to figure out a way to get away from Maureen for a little while," he whispered.

"What's wrong? Marital bliss over already?" Brandon had to tease him. It was too fun not to. Maureen and George were like give-you-a-toothache in love. Maureen was pregnant for the third time, and they were always doing shit as a family.

"Nothing's wrong. She's home here with the kids, and I thought it's been a long time since we did anything." He lowered his voice even more. "It's been a difficult pregnancy and I'm doing what I can to help, but there's only so much I can take on for her. She's in bed with Jason and Lacy, and my hands have cramped from rubbing her feet. So, do you want to go out for a drink? I could use one."

"You can't leave Maureen like that!"

"She's got the kids in bed and told me to get out of the house because she can't stand to see my face right now. So I'm going to take that as a sign of liberation for a few hours. I can meet you at Whitehall's in a half hour if you're up for it."

"Sure." Brandon was already heading to his closet. "I'll be there."

"Great. You're saving my life, man."

"Okay, but you can't drink much, because I'm not carrying you home and pouring your ass in bed like I did when we were roommates." That had been a trip. George hadn't been a huge drinker, but man, when he had, he'd really done it up right.

"Duh. Maureen would kick my ass if I came home drunk. I think I just need a few kid-free hours. Thanks."

They ended the call, and Brandon changed his clothes into something he hadn't spent the day working in. "I'm meeting George for a while," he told his grandma, who was comfortable in her favorite chair and had her feet up. "I won't be late." He leaned down to hug her, then went out to his car and headed toward downtown.

Whitehall's was a western sort of place. Not a bar for the tourists, but a real kind of neighborhood bar that had been there for decades. There were pictures of horses and cowboys because they had been patrons at some point—not the horses, but their owners. The inside had been wood-paneled years ago, and now it was dark from decades of smoke, hands, and people. The place smelled of beer with a faint hint of lingering cigarette smoke. Brandon looked around and spotted George toward the wall at one of the long, worn tables with benches on each side.

"Hey," Brandon said as George stood. They hugged tightly and then sat back down. George already had a beer in front of him, and Brandon went to the bar and returned. "So what's really going on?"

George took a gulp of his beer. "Maureen is having a hard time with this one. The last two pregnancies she pretty much sailed right through. She was uncomfortable, but she just kept on going. This one has her tired all the time and in some pain. She isn't sleeping at night and gets up to pee every five minutes. First she's starved, and then she doesn't want to eat and the scent of food makes her sick." He set his mug down hard, banging it on the table.

"Well. Not every pregnancy is easy. Maybe she was lucky with the last two and is paying for it with this one." Not that he was any kind of expert. The closest he wanted to come to pregnancy and giving birth was holding the baby once they brought it home. "Jeez, man, you just got to be there for her."

"I know." George looked around. "I just need a bit of time and things will be cool. Sometimes the worry and stress get to be a little much." At least he wasn't guzzling his beer and ordering another right away. That was a really good sign.

"Would you guys like something to eat?" the waitress, Shirley, asked. "Oh, hey, Brandon." She smiled at him. "How you been?"

Brandon returned her greeting and stood so they could share a hug. "Not bad. It's been a long time." In high school Shirley had been a close friend and knew he was gay, though he never told her. Shirley had guessed, and she had been his fake girlfriend for a time. They'd even gone to prom together and had had a blast.

She nodded when he stepped back. "How are your folks?" she asked, and Brandon shrugged. "That bad?"

"Yeah. How long have you been working here?"

"About six months." She grinned and flashed a ring.

"Congratulations!" Brandon said, giving her another hug.

"Ashton Martin and I have been dating for a couple years now, and he asked me to marry him. I only work here a couple nights a week so I can help save for the wedding." She bounced on her heels.

"That's awesome. Do you know George?" Brandon said, making a quick introduction. "His wife is expecting their third child and this is his night away, so he needs another beer and plenty of junk food."

Shirley rolled her eyes. "Ashton says he wants to have kids right away, but I told him we'd wait a little." She grinned.

"Smart woman," George said, then held up his hands. "Don't get me wrong. I love my wife and the kids, but if we had it to do over, we'd probably wait a little longer."

Brandon rolled his eyes. It was easy for him to say that, but Maureen was a devout Catholic, and not having kids meant George wasn't going to be having sex. And somehow Brandon thought that wasn't an option. Though after number three....

He and George told Shirley what they wanted to eat.

"I'll put your orders in and bring another round." She hurried away, and Brandon settled back in his seat, sipping from his glass.

"She seems nice."

"I can't believe you never met," Brandon said as he looked around the bar to see who else was there. In a town like this, where he'd lived most of his life, there were always people he knew around.

"Who's the guy sitting uncomfortably at the bar? He looks like he stepped out of *GQ* and doesn't have a clue here," George said, tilting his head to the right.

Brandon followed his gaze and stifled a gasp. "That's my new boss." Brandon wondered what Thomas was doing here. This didn't seem like his kind of place, though he didn't know of many fancy martini bars in town.

"Boss?" George cocked his eyebrows upward.

"His mom and my grandma know each other. Thomas just moved to town and needed an assistant. And since I can't seem to get anyone to take a second look at me, I took the job. He's a pretty nice guy, but is a little clueless about stuff." Brandon leaned closer. "He doesn't do his own shopping or even laundry."

George shrugged. "It's not like there's Safeway in New York City. I suppose he's one of those works-all-the-time people?" He shook his head. "I can't see doing that any more than I have to. I like what I do all right, but I like the time I spend at home so much more." He took another drink and pulled out his phone. Brandon knew he was about to be shown a series of kid pictures. Grumble all he wanted, but George was a doting father.

"Maybe that's the difference between you and him. He has all the money he could possibly want, but no one else. And you have a family and are eternally broke." Brandon watched as Thomas leaned on the bar with a beer, and stood. "I'm going to ask if he wants to join us."

"Good, maybe he'll buy a round."

"George!" Brandon hissed. "That's tacky."

George rolled his eyes. "I'm the broke father of three. Anyone buying the drinks is welcome, and let me tell you, pride went out the window a long time ago." He set down his glass, and Brandon sighed as he made his way across the room to where Thomas sat.

"Are you getting dinner?" Brandon asked.

Thomas seemed startled, like he was surprised someone would talk to him. In the time since Brandon had seen him, no one other than the bartender had paid him any attention. "Brandon. Yeah. There was no food in the house, and I thought…." He shrugged.

"My friend and I are right over there at that table. You're welcome to join us instead of sitting alone." Brandon stepped back, letting Thomas make up his own mind. "Did you order food?"

"Yeah. A while ago. I think the kitchen must be a little backed up." Thomas cradled his beer mug. "I'd like to join you if that's really okay."

Brandon caught the bartender's eye. "Stan, can you send his food to the table over there?" He pointed, and Stan nodded, raising a hand before going back to pulling beers. The place was getting busier as the evening wore on. "Come on." He motioned, and Thomas got up off the stool and followed him over to the table.

"George Hanson, Thomas Stepford," Brandon said, and the two of them shook hands.

Thomas sat down, and Brandon sat on the bench next to him.

"Are you new in town?" George asked.

"New back in town, I guess, is accurate. I moved here from New York, but grew up here," Thomas explained.

"That's cool. Do you have family here?"

"My parents and brother. That's part of why I moved back. Mom and Dad are getting older and need some help. With telecommuting and the internet, I can do most of what I did in New York from here."

"Do you like it?" George took a sip from his glass.

"Pretty much so far." Thomas emptied his glass and lifted it. Shirley hurried over and took his order. Thomas explained that he had a tab at the bar, and she said she'd arrange to transfer it. "It's a nice enough place, but different. Almost too quiet."

George snorted softly. "Then come on over to my house. I have two kids, one eighteen months and the other a little over three. Maureen is expecting our third, so there's never any time that's quiet except the middle of the night, and even then the kids will be up wanting something. Believe me, you can have all the noise you could possibly want."

Thomas chuckled. "No thanks." The two of them clinked glasses. "Better you than me. The good thing about being gay is that I don't have to worry about accidental kids. Of course, unless I really want them, and then I have to go through hell to get them." Thomas shook his head.

"Do you want kids?" Brandon asked, and Thomas paused as though he'd never been asked that question before.

"I don't think so," Thomas answered quietly. "I never gave that part of my life much thought really."

"Why not?" George asked.

The words had been on the tip of Brandon's tongue, but he was glad George had asked for him. Brandon was very curious about the answer. Heck, he was curious about anything related to Thomas. The man had certainly captured his attention, and Brandon had a difficult time looking away from him, let alone not hanging on every word. It was stupid and he knew it. Thomas was his boss, and he needed to maintain a professional distance. Thomas might have just admitted that he was gay and all, but that didn't mean he was interested in Brandon. God, things were getting messed up in his head.

"Well," Thomas began, "I had big plans that kids didn't fit into." He gulped his beer, and Brandon wondered if he was getting up some Dutch courage.

Shirley came over with their food and asked if he wanted another, and Thomas nodded.

"We didn't have much growing up, and when I was a teenager, I wanted a car… like most kids do when they get their license. Mom and Dad couldn't afford to get one for me. Not back then. They were working too hard to make ends meet. So I worked and bought my own."

"Grandma told me about your lawn-mowing business," Brandon said. "She seemed really impressed."

Thomas smiled as his beer arrived, and he took a drink. "I found out I was good at business and making money. I started selling candy out of my locker at school, and then other things. After I graduated from high school, I used the money I'd saved to buy some inexpensive properties that I rented to students and then used that money to buy more. I had a lot of cash coming in and was able to support myself. From there I put together some larger deals and made more money. But each deal took a lot of time and meeting with a lot of people. I loved it, and eventually I moved to New York, where I put together massive deals that made even more money." Thomas grinned. "I was so proud of myself, and my parents were proud—everyone was." He stared at his plate and began to eat, growing quiet. "I shouldn't brag."

"You weren't," George told him. "You were telling a story."

Brandon worried a little about Thomas. He seemed upset, gulping down his beer and asking for another. He'd need to slow down if he wasn't going to get drunk, but it seemed that maybe that was Thomas's aim.

"Well, New York, and the business environment there, is very cutthroat and requires a lot of time. I went at it tooth and nail and made a lot of money and helped build a lot of buildings. But…." Thomas looked up from his plate, wiping his fingers on a napkin. "Guys, everything comes at a price. Believe me."

"I understand that…," George said.

Brandon snickered. "Who knows that better than you? Every time you have sex, your wife gets pregnant and you end up with another kid."

"Have you ever heard of birth control?" Thomas asked.

"Maureen is very religious." Brandon picked up one of his wings, waving it around for a second.

"Religion or not, I think I'm taking things into my own hands after this. She's having such a hard time right now."

Brandon turned to Thomas, and both of them cracked up. Brandon dropped his wing on his plate, laughing like hell. "I think you'll have to." He could barely see straight, and even George laughed when he realized what he'd said.

"I meant a vasectomy." He rolled his eyes, and Thomas snorted, sending Brandon into more peals of laughter. God, he wondered for a second if they'd all had too much to drink. He noted that he needed to switch to soda after this glass, because the way the others were going, he was going to need to get them all home.

"Sure you did," Thomas teased.

"He'll have three kids under four, and two of them in diapers. I think that's enough birth control for anyone." Brandon had stopped laughing.

"Sometimes I wish I'd had kids," Thomas said rather morosely. "I'm almost forty and spent a lot of my time working. That's part of why I came here. I want to have a life again." Thomas drank half his beer and really seemed to be going on a tear. He asked Shirley for another. She brought it, along with a glass of water. Thankfully Thomas drank some of both and went back to eating for a while.

Brandon shared a look with George, who seemed unconcerned. "You can do whatever you want. You know that. Hell, you're proof of it," Brandon told Thomas. "You set out to do things most people only dream about while they sit at home in front of the television, watching one of those shows where rich people bicker and fight with each other."

"Maureen loves those *Real Housewives* shows. She says it makes it look like rich people are just like us… or some such rot. Personally I think it makes everyone look ridiculous. I can't stand it for a second, but she loves it."

"See. You lived that life and made something of yourself," Brandon said. Part of him wished he could be in Thomas's shoes, successful and with enough money that he could take care of his grandma instead of her helping him.

"Yes, I did." Thomas turned to him, his eyes deepening. "I had goals and I fulfilled them, more than. I became a huge success." There wasn't a hint of happiness in Thomas's eyes, and that sent a chill through Brandon. It was like Thomas was empty in a way… or believed he was.

"So after reaching one dream, you need to find another," Brandon offered, then blushed when it came out sounding like he was some idealistic little kid. He turned away and ate some of his wings. He figured if he was busy, he wouldn't say something stupid again. But damn it all, he kept glancing at Thomas, who had finished yet another beer and ordered another in a relatively short period of time.

"I'm going to hit the head," George said, getting up and leaving Brandon alone with Thomas.

"Are they good?" Brandon asked, glancing at the last of the wings.

"Yeah." Thomas dropped the bones on the plate, wiped his hands, drank some more of his beer, then set the glass aside, pushing it away. "I think I've had enough. Blaze, a friend from back in New York, tells me I get maudlin when I've been drinking, and I think I'm there." He drained the glass of water and burped, covering his mouth with his hand.

"I'll drive you home and I can arrange to pick up your car in the morning." Brandon finished the last of his dinner as George returned. He caught Shirley's attention, and she brought some coffee and another soda.

"I got the check," Thomas said, pulling out a large bill and handing it to Shirley when she returned. "Thanks for everything." He pressed it into her hand and then got up. Brandon wondered just how long Thomas had been sitting at the bar before they got there, because he was pretty unsteady on his feet.

"Is that enough?" Brandon asked Shirley as Thomas rocked his way toward the door.

"Yeah. More than…."

"Okay. Keep the change." Brandon smiled. "Put it toward the wedding." They shared a smile. "I'll see you later," he said to George.

"Yeah, I need to get back to Maureen." He pulled Brandon into a hug. "It was good to see you."

"You good to drive?"

"Yeah. I'm fine," George said, and Brandon looked him in the eyes, making George chuckle. "I didn't drink all the beers I ordered. Thomas downed two of them before I even got hold of them. He's the one you need to worry about. I only had two, and plenty of food. I'm good." George went to his car and seemed okay.

Brandon hurried to Thomas, who was fussing with his shirt. "This way." He guided Thomas to his car and got him inside. "Give me your keys," Brandon said, and Thomas handed them over. "You can't drive."

"I'd get a cab at home," Thomas grumbled. "No cabs here."

"You just have to call them." And somehow Brandon doubted Thomas would be able to think well enough to make that call. "It's okay. I'm going to take you home." He got Thomas buckled in before pulling out of the parking lot.

"I don't have any friends here," Thomas said as he stared out the window. "I grew up here, but I don't know anybody. Not really." He turned his head toward Brandon, and he seemed to be trying to focus. "I called people I knew once, but things are different… everything is different."

"Things are the same here. It's you who's different."

"I know that," Thomas snapped and then cringed. "I'm sorry. I know I changed. I became one of those New York people." He hung his head, which bounced a little with each bump in the road. "I used to go to Whitehall's when I was in college. It was a favorite. Knew everybody." At least that explained why Thomas had been there. "Shit changes, I guess."

After a few minutes, Brandon pulled in to Thomas's drive and up to the door. He looked over at Thomas, who leaned back in the seat, sighing. "How much did you have to drink?" Thomas seemed very drunk, and it worried him.

"What you saw. Was always a lightweight," Thomas slurred.

Brandon got out and went around to help Thomas out of the car and into the house. The stairs provided an interesting navigational challenge. "Come on, Thomas. You can make it up." He was already starting to get sleepy, and Brandon patted Thomas's stubbled cheek. "You need to get upstairs." He pushed, and Thomas started going again. Brandon got him to the room he'd made up earlier, pulled down the covers, and got Thomas seated on the side of the bed. "Can you get your shoes and stuff off? I'm going to get you some aspirin and water so you don't feel so bad in the morning." Brandon hurried to the bathroom and got what he needed.

Thomas had flopped back on the bed by the time he returned, already snoring away. Brandon pulled him up and got him to take the pills and drink the water. Then Thomas collapsed on the mattress, and in seconds he snored loud enough to wake the dead.

Brandon took off Thomas's shoes and socks, and swung his legs around so they were up in the bed. Then he opened Thomas's shirt and rolled him from side to side to get it off. He gasped at a large straight scar down Thomas's shoulder to his chest. It was pink and old, but Brandon wondered what could have happened. Brandon had to stop his finger from tracing it, but his gaze raked over the rest of him.

Thomas was beautiful. He didn't look the same as the first time Brandon had seen him without his shirt. He looked older, but in a good way, like his body had seen life. There was the scar and other marks, but Thomas still seemed just strong, and even more solid than he'd been then. Brandon wanted to touch, but he felt like a perv, and he'd never been given permission to touch. Hell, he wanted to know what those muscles felt like under his hands, though.

Slowly Thomas rolled over with a groan, and Brandon stepped back. He pulled the covers over Thomas, then left the room and locked the house behind him before going back to his grandma's.

"YOU'RE STILL up?" Brandon asked when he found his grandma in the living room under a blanket in her favorite chair, feet up and television on.

"Can't sleep." She turned to him. "Don't get old—it sucks. Half the time you're too tired to do anything, and the rest of the time you can't sleep." She tugged the blanket up, and Brandon sat on the sofa. "Did you have a good time?"

"In a way. I was at Whitehall's with George, and Thomas was there."

"Your boss Thomas?" she clarified and Brandon nodded.

"I think he's really lonely." Brandon looked down at his shoes.

"Well, he wouldn't know many people here now, I suspect."

Brandon took her closest hand. "I think what I saw was something that goes deeper than just the few days since he's been here. I think he's alone and has been for a while. Anyway, we all talked, and Thomas drank enough that I took him home and put him to bed." He sighed. "What do I do?"

His grandma didn't say anything right away, thinking as she usually did for important questions. "You're his assistant and you can help organize his life and make it easier, but I don't think part of your job description is his mental health." She leaned forward a little.

"I know that. But should I ask him about it in the morning?" Brandon wondered if he should call Marjorie and ask.

His grandma licked her lips. "No. I think you should say nothing to him. He may be embarrassed about what he said, and he deserves his privacy. Do your job. If you want to watch so you know he's okay, do that. The man has his pride, and he was out for a drink with you guys. He blew off a little steam and maybe he said some things he isn't proud of. I think a good assistant would keep that to himself and just go ahead and do his job." She sat back in her chair as though she'd said her piece. "You should go on to bed. Morning comes early when you have to go to work."

Brandon shrugged, kissed his grandma good night, and went to his room. Even though he wasn't expecting anything from Thomas, he checked his phone and then cleaned up and climbed in bed. He hoped he'd go right to sleep, but he had a feeling that old fantasies were going to crop up plenty during the night.

Chapter 5

THOMAS PRIED his eyes open, groaning as he lifted his head off the pillow. He heard soft noises in the house and smelled coffee, which made his stomach roll over and threaten to go on strike for the rest of his life. "Just leave me to die," he moaned to no one, which spiked the reason he'd been drinking in the first place. Sometimes he was so pathetic.

He pulled the pillow over his head to block out the light and closed his eyes once again. His mouth tasted like he'd been sucking a tail pipe, and the smell of his breath made him nauseous.

"Thomas." The voice was quiet, but it sounded like yelling. "I brought you something to drink."

"Just go away," he grumped and slowly rolled over, thinking his head was going to explode with each movement.

"Fine. You're the boss. But I think it's fair to warn you that the men are coming this morning to unpack those crates in the living room, and they're going to bring tools. It isn't going to be pretty."

"Oh, fuck a duck," Thomas said, pushing back the covers, keeping his eyes closed as he slowly sat up.

Brandon pressed a glass into his hand, and he drank a little. Pills were pushed into his grip, and he took them, swallowing the juice. At least the stuff made his mouth less nasty for a little while.

"Go and take a shower. I have some water that I'm putting beside your bed. Drink all of it—the fluids will make you feel better." Brandon left the room, and Thomas finished the juice and drank the water, then stumbled into the bathroom.

He turned on the water but not the lights and stepped into the shower, holding the tile to make sure he stayed upright. Every drop felt like it pelted his skin, at least at first. Then his muscles relaxed and he sighed, letting the heat crash over him. Finally he washed up and shampooed his hair, rinsed well, and got out of the shower. The room was cold, and he shivered until he dried off and brushed his damn teeth. Now at least he felt halfway to human, and went to get dressed.

Thomas schlumped down the stairs and shuffled into the kitchen with his eyes still half-lidded. Brandon pushed a mug of coffee across the counter. "Thank you. God, remind me never to take a drink again." He held his head as he sat at the kitchen table. "I feel like I got hit by a truck."

"You were sucking down those beers pretty fast last night." Brandon left him alone, going into the other room, then returning. "I'm off to the store to get some food in this house, and this afternoon I have some interviews with housekeepers." He turned to him. "We could go the easy way and use Merry Maids. They're a service that will come in on a scheduled basis and do what you want them to."

Thomas sipped the coffee and groaned. "Go ahead and use them. I'm not a huge mess-maker, and having someone reliable is important. Make sure they can do special engagements. If I have to entertain, stuff like that."

"No problem. I'll handle it and review the details with you later." Brandon turned to leave the house, and Thomas wished for the millionth time that he'd switched to something else to drink last night, especially when his phone rang and he cradled his throbbing head. He should have put it on vibrate.

"Blaze…," he groused.

"Damn, you sound like hell. What did you do?" Blaze seemed as chipper as they came.

"Well, I went out for dinner because there was nothing in the house. And… my new assistant and a friend of his asked me to join them, and I drank too much." He sipped his coffee and let the quiet of the house and the caffeine do their work.

Blaze chuckled. "Why did you do that? I haven't known you to drink too much in years."

Thomas sighed. "I think I was lonely and feeling a little sorry for myself last night, and drinking only made things worse."

"It usually does." Blaze paused. "Are you sure that's all there is to it?" Sometimes Blaze had an insight that startled him. "I heard Marjorie hired you an assistant and that he's cute and...."

Thomas's hangover dissipated, at least from his immediate consciousness. "Sometimes I swear that woman is a menace."

Blaze laughed loudly. "I've been telling you that for years. She knows everything. Thankfully she keeps most things to herself."

"Dang her," Thomas swore.

"So is there an issue with your assistant?" Blaze asked, and Thomas growled. "I'm going to take that as a yes. Now. You can either tell me what's got you tied in knots, or I'll worm it out of you with texts and re-minders of your hangover. Just make it easy on your-self and come clean."

"There's no issue. Brandon is handsome, and I think he's going to be very good at his job." Thomas scratched the back of his head, wishing like hell that he could get out of this conversation. Maybe some-one would take out Blaze's cell tower... not pretty, but preferable to going down the road he was being led.

"Thomas...," Blaze coaxed. "I can fill in the blanks on my own if you don't want to talk about it."

"You're a real dick, you know that?" Thomas snapped.

"And I like dick, so that comes in handy," Blaze quipped, and Thomas rolled his eyes.

"Ass," he retorted because he was too hungover for pithy comebacks. "I don't want to talk about this."

"Which only means there's something to talk about." Blaze could be as stubborn as a mule, as stub-born... as Thomas was. "Just spill it."

"Fine...," he huffed. "Brandon was the kid who used to mow my lawn for me."

"And you perved on lawn-mower boy?" Blaze was clearly having too much fun with this. "That's pretty sick, man."

"I did not. He was fifteen. I barely noticed him then, and now he's grown into a stunning man and he keeps looking at me... that way. Like he's interested." Thomas swallowed and then drank some more coffee.

"You know that doesn't matter unless...." Blaze practically cackled. "Are you interested?"

"I'm not dead. Brandon is gorgeous, and he has a good heart and...." Thomas wished to hell he had never allowed this conversation to start. "He lives with his grandmother and needed this job so he could help take care of her. How many twenty-five-year-old kids have that kind of patience and care in them?"

"You like this kid... and that's why you were getting drunk?" Blaze pressed.

"Yes and no. I like him, but that's all there is to it and all there will ever be." Thomas stood, and his head swirled. He slowly sat back down and waited for the room to stop spinning. "It doesn't matter what my personal feelings are or may be... or the way he looks at me.... Nothing is ever going to come of it."

"Please. This isn't the damn fifties. You have no one to apologize to or ask permission of. You're the boss, and if you want to date your assistant and he's agreeable, then do it."

"No. I'm not going down the same road as I did with Angus. That isn't going to happen!" He spoke loud enough that he gave himself a headache. "I was drinking last night because I was a little lonely, and then Brandon came over and—"

"You continued drinking because you're interested in him and you were too chicken to say anything and tried to bury your feelings in the bottom of a glass. How did that work out for you?"

"Dammit, Blaze!" He was having too much fun at his expense.

"No. You need to stop repressing any feelings you might have for anyone because of what Angus did to you. I know that asshole hurt you bad, but you can't stay away from everyone because of him. The man was a complete jerk, and he's paying for what he did and will for some time yet. I don't care if you're interested in your assistant or the guy who lives down the street. But as your friend, I hate to see you shutting yourself up behind work and anything else you can think of so you don't have to deal with anyone who might hurt you."

"I've always been too busy for a relationship," Thomas said.

"You keep telling yourself that. But I think that excuse is starting to sound hollow, even to you." Blaze paused, and papers shuffled in the background. "Anyway, I called to give you a brief update. Everything is going great here. The projects are on schedule, and I've been told the permits are in the mail. We are all set."

"That's good. What are our next projects?" Thomas asked.

"There are a number of proposals that have been put forward, and I've scheduled a meeting for later in the week to review them. Marjorie has it on your calendar—she's sending you the details. Relax a little and take it easy. That's why you went out there in the first place."

"Tell me about it." Thomas could only sit around watching television for so long. If he was going to take it easy and step back from work, then he needed things to occupy his time, but he hadn't found anything yet. Not that he'd actually been looking.

"Ask your assistant for ideas on some things you can do. He lives there," Blaze offered, and Thomas rolled his eyes.

"Just take care of the things in the office and let me worry about my personal life." He was feeling snippy, and the more Blaze pushed, the grouchier he was becoming.

"I'm your friend, so I care about both sides of you, remember?" Blaze's voice hardened. If they were in the same room, they'd probably be standing toe-to-toe, arms crossed, staring at each other until one of them looked away.

"Fine. Let me know if there's anything you need." Thomas ended the call and slid his phone on the counter, lucky it didn't fall and smash on the floor. Not that he cared at the moment. He was put out and angry with Blaze, and if he were honest, with himself. Why did he always seem to be interested in people he wasn't supposed to get involved with?

Not that it mattered. He was *not* going to develop romantic feelings for his assistant. That was simply too cliché for words. Thomas finished his coffee, feeling more human by the second, and then went upstairs to change into the clothes he intended to wear for the day.

"THOMAS," BRANDON called from the front as Thomas came down the stairs. "I got your groceries. And I snagged your keys, and a friend helped me get your car back."

Thomas met him in the kitchen, where Brandon had begun putting things away.

"I went ahead and got you some staple sort of things, as well as what you asked for. I hope that's okay." Brandon put everything from the bags away, then hurried back outside and returned with another load.

"How much did you get?" Thomas asked, peeking in the bags.

"There was nothing at all here, so I bought some basics that won't go bad. At least you aren't going to starve." Brandon smiled, and Thomas paused because, damn, the sun came out when he did that.

Thomas forced himself to turn away. He'd just told Blaze he wasn't going to get involved with his assistant, and a smile had him forgetting all about that within seconds.

"I got you some ice cream. I wasn't sure about flavor, so I went with chocolate, and some sorbet in case you liked that." Brandon continued putting things away as he talked. "I got pasta and stuff to make sauce. I didn't know if you liked that, but it's easy to make." He stretched up to put the pasta in the cupboard.

Thomas's attention focused on the strip of skin that now showed just above Brandon's belt. He took a step closer, his fingers tingling to touch. He paused, blinking, and turned away.

"Thomas, are you okay?" Brandon said gently, closing the cupboard doors. "Maybe you need to lie down for a while and get the alcohol out of your system. You seem really distracted."

"Sorry," Thomas said, realizing he hadn't been listening. "You were saying?"

Brandon cleared his throat. "I was asking if you can cook." He turned to finish getting the refrigerated things put away. "I called the maid service while I was out, and they were very nice. They said they'd send someone by tomorrow. I can talk to them if you'd like. I had a few other calls to make about cleaning ladies, but if it's okay, we can see if the service works out first."

"All right." Thomas shrugged. He didn't have a preference. "That's fine on the maid service, and as for the cooking part, not really. In New York I mainly bought my dinners or heated things up. I didn't have time to make huge meals or things like that. I don't burn water, but I never learned to cook very well."

"Okay." Brandon closed the refrigerator door, picked up a tablet from the counter, and opened it to review his handwritten list. "The people will be here to unpack those crates for you soon. Can I ask what's in them?"

"Two works of art that are very important to me. Maybe you can help me find a place for them. I don't want to put either of them over the fireplace. That's the worst location because of the heat and then cold."

Brandon looked around. "I'd suggest putting them in the family room, but it's open to the kitchen, and that means cooking steam and stuff. How about the dining room, or the living room away from the fireplace? It isn't like you'll be building a fire anytime soon."

"All right. I'd like to keep them somewhere I can see them."

"I understand that," Brandon said and wandered out of the room.

Thomas pushed back from the table and went after him. He found Brandon in the living room.

"We could put one here, but I think it might get some direct sun and we don't want that. It might fade." Brandon walked through the room, looking at each wall, shaking his head. "I don't like it in here."

Thomas laughed. "I don't either. This room doesn't feel comfortable, and with the huge windows, it seems like a fishbowl."

"And those curtains." Brandon shivered. "They're way too heavy and froofy. If you were going to buy this place, I'd help you pick out something else, but it doesn't make sense to spend money on something when you're only going to be here a few months." He sighed and continued on, wandering into the dining room.

"I thought the de Kooning might go here. I always had it near this table at my place in New York." Thomas scoped out the blank space. It would be the perfect size for it. He nodded, imagining the bright colors on the wall.

Brandon spun around, his mouth hanging open and eyes wide. "A real one? Wow. Awesome." He bit his lip and visibly forced himself to move on. "You could try the hall for the other one, but with the front door, I don't think so." They both wandered into the family room. "We could hang it here." Brandon indicated the wall behind the sofa. "It's away from the kitchen, and you can see it from the chairs. Either that or over there, opposite the television. Both are interior walls and won't get direct sun."

"I think either of them will work." Thomas liked that it would be in a room he would use often. The works held a great deal of sentimental value for him. "Once they're unpacked, we can choose."

"Excellent. You said they were valuable, so I contacted a local gallery. They are going to send someone over tomorrow to hang them for you." Brandon really seemed on the ball. "I didn't think you'd want us hanging them with wire and a nail."

"That's very good." Thomas smiled, spinning to Brandon as he turned to him. "You seem to understand what I need before I do sometimes." He stilled, and Brandon did the same.

Brandon licked his lips, and Thomas stifled a groan. Hell and blast. Marjorie had developed a sense of anticipating what he needed, but she did it over years of working together, and here Brandon was doing it within days. It was so intimate so fast. Not only that, but the naked heat in his gaze—granted, it had only lasted a few seconds—made Thomas's knees weak.

"Thank you." Thomas turned and strode out of the room, heading for the stairs. He needed some time alone to clear his damned head and get those thoughts of Brandon out of there.

Upstairs, he went right to the bathroom to splash cold water on his face. He really wanted to take a cold shower to make his errant dick stop aching in his jeans. He sure as hell hoped Brandon hadn't seen the bulge. The last thing he wanted was for Brandon to see his arousal and either take it as an invitation, or be horrified and decide he didn't want to work with him any longer.

Two fucking days. That's all it had taken. Two days and he was already having thoughts about Brandon that he shouldn't be having, like wondering what was under his polo shirt, and with the tantalizing glimpses of skin, he was....

No. Thomas wiped his face, thinking unsexy thoughts. He closed his eyes, breathed evenly, and shifted his mind to business deals and the paperwork Blaze had sent him to review. That sent his mind in a completely different direction and cleared out images of Brandon.

The chime of an incoming message interrupted his thoughts. *The man is here to unpack the crates.*

Thomas responded that he'd be down in a few minutes and dried his face before leaving the bathroom.

"Be careful and take your time. These are delicate items," Brandon was saying as the whine of tools drifted to Thomas's ears and continued as he reached the room. One man was in the living room on his knees, removing screws from the first case.

"That's great. Thank you," Thomas told the man in coveralls, who looked about his age.

"No problem," he said, barely looking up from his work. "How much do you want me to do?" He removed the last screw and lifted off the wooden cover to reveal paper and Bubble Wrap. "I can take off more if you want."

Brandon set the covers out of the way against the wall.

"I think that's good. We're having them hung tomorrow, so they can stay that way until we're ready for them. I know this is a piddly job, but I didn't have the tools for it." He turned to Brandon, who nodded confirmation.

"It's no problem." He opened the second case and then packed up the tools. "If you need anything else, just give us a call." He smiled and nodded before closing the door after himself.

"I'm anxious to see them again, but I don't want to take any chances," Thomas said, feeling a little like an excited kid. In the end he left them where they were and wandered back through the house. He didn't have any meetings and wasn't sure what he wanted to do. Having time on his hands was unusual for him, and he didn't know what to do to fill it. He ended up staring at the still-packed paintings, his eyes unfocused as he worked things through.

"Umm... I should go through the house and see what other things you might need." Brandon left the room, and Thomas's gaze followed him before he could chastise himself for it.

"How many things are on that list of yours?" Thomas asked.

"Not many," Brandon said, pausing. "I need to call Marjorie to see if she has anything she needs me to follow up on. I was also going to run some loads of laundry. The cleaning service will do that as part of their contract, but I figured I'd take care of it until they start. I wondered, do you have anything that needs to be done?"

"There are some clothes to take to the cleaners." Thomas followed Brandon as he left. "They're in my room. I'll bring them down. I like to have my shirts professionally cleaned so they're crisp."

"No problem." Brandon went into the kitchen, and Thomas heard the dishwasher start. When he went upstairs after detouring to his office to get his phone, he stopped in his bathroom, passing Brandon as he carried his dirty towels away. "Just trying to keep everything cleaned for you."

Thomas got his shirts and brought them to the laundry room, where Brandon took charge of them while he spoke with Marjorie.

"Sounds good. I'm just getting things together here. I need to make another run to the store for supplies. I got him groceries, but not cleaning stuff and extra paper products. The house is pretty much set up. We aren't going to hang most of the pictures unless Thomas changes his mind." Brandon smiled, pinking a little, probably because he was talking about him. Thomas shrugged. He knew Brandon was talking to Marjorie, who knew most of his secrets. "They're coming to hang the paintings tomorrow. ... When does he have meetings?"

Thomas cocked his head as Brandon listened.

"Okay. So I'm pretty much up to date. This afternoon I was going to make him some things that he can reheat so he has some meals in the house." Brandon listened again, and then he smiled and ended the call.

"What did Marjorie say?" Thomas crossed his arms over his chest.

"That I'm being very good to you, and that cooking is above and beyond." Brandon smiled. "I think she likes me."

Thomas snickered. "I think she does too." He looked at the lined-up laundry soap on the shelf. "I was wondering what there is to do here. I have time on my hands and don't know what to do." Thomas put his hands on his hips. "I grew up here, but I don't think we ever did much. There are a bunch of touristy things around, but we never did them."

"Well… there's Pikes Peak, but that's an all-day thing to get to the top. There's Cripple Creek. It's maybe an hour from town. It's the old gold-mining town, and there are a lot of things to do there—tours, shops, even some shows, and a saloon and old-time reenactments. It's the Old West at its best because it's real… well, mostly real. I think there's a train through town as well. I haven't been there since I was in school, but I can look it up and see what you need tickets for." Brandon got busy immediately, checking things on his phone. "There are plenty of tickets available, especially for one."

"Two," Thomas said. "I don't want to go all the way up there alone, so if you don't mind, you can come with me. That is, if you'd like to." Sure, he wanted to do something and didn't relish the thought of spending the entire day alone, but he should have tried to find someone who he wasn't having feelings for that he shouldn't have. God, Brandon even made his thoughts convoluted.

"It sounds like fun." Brandon's smile was genuine and warm.

"Awesome."

"I can reserve two sets of tickets for the train. The other things we'll have to figure out once we get there. When did you want to go?"

"We can leave soon," Thomas said. He'd made the invitation, so he wasn't going to take it back.

"I have the directions all set up in my phone, and I'll get some water and a few snacks so we have things. I can go to Costco later tonight." It was curious how Brandon rearranged his day but didn't lose sight of the things he needed to do.

Thomas got a jacket just in case, and Brandon brought a small cooler and followed him out of the house. They went to Thomas's car and buckled up before heading out of town and into the mountains.

"What are you doing?" Thomas asked as Brandon typed on his phone.

"Letting Marjorie know we'll be out of pocket for a while. She can probably text, but cell service is most likely a little spotty." He was being a good assistant, but Thomas wasn't sure how much he wanted Marjorie to know. "I'm not giving her any details, just that we may be unreachable."

Once finished, Brandon set the phone on his lap and gave him directions as needed. It took about an hour to get there, passing through some amazing mountain scenery.

"Sometimes I forget how breathtaking it can be here," Thomas said as he slowed down, taking a curve near a deep drop-off. "There's nothing like this in New York."

"Nope." Brandon smiled. "I always liked it here. As a teenager, I used to love to drive up into the mountains just to see what there was to see. I got to the top of Pikes Peak for a field trip in junior high. I had great teachers who thought enough to use the natural beauty around us in their lessons."

Thomas glanced over, his breath hitching at the beauty and pure joy in Brandon's eyes. He turned back to the front, navigating the mountain road until they crossed into the old mining region with the town in the valley. Multicolored slag heaps from played-out mines colored the mountainsides around the town. They were a beautiful reminder of what was done to get at the gold in the Rocky Mountains. Thomas turned into the parking lot, and after paying, he found a spot and got out of the car.

"Wow, this place is cool," Thomas said half under his breath. "It looks like a step out of time." He swiveled his head, trying to take it all in. "Do you want to wander through town?"

"Sure," Brandon answered, and they left the parking lot. The town did indeed look like something out of another era, with the old storefronts and saloons. "Oh," Brandon said quietly. "They're casinos. A lot of them." He sounded disappointed. "I forgot that they went into gambling in a big way up here. There were a few of them that had been here a while, but I don't remember this many." He sighed, disappointment clouding his expression. "This used to be a really quiet, sort of living museum." Some of the light went out of his eyes, and Brandon bit his lower lip.

Thomas couldn't help sharing some of Brandon's disappointment. "Maybe we can go to the station and ride the train like we planned?"

"Yeah." Brandon gave himself a shake and led the way.

The train station did look like something from the nineteenth century, and the brightly painted train pulled in, making Brandon smile. Thomas wasn't supposed to get so wrapped up in Brandon's reactions, but it was hard not to. Thomas was finding it difficult to keep his distance.

"Let me take care of the tickets," he said, approaching the window and giving his name. He paid for the tickets Brandon had reserved, and they waited in line for boarding, along with a throng of tourists. "Lots of people."

"It's tourist season," Brandon said, lightly bumping his shoulder. "That's okay. For today you and I can be tourists and have some fun." He was practically bouncing again, and Thomas couldn't help but share in his enthusiasm.

They boarded the train and found seats next to each other as the others filed on, filling the car. As they pulled away from the town and the casinos, they slowly wound up and through the mountains, where the abandoned and ghostly remains of gold-mining history passed outside.

"The slag heaps," Brandon said, pointing.

"Yeah. They dumped the dirt just outside the mines," Thomas said, and the recorded narration told of companies who came in to work the old slag heaps in search of missed gold, sometimes finding gold themselves. "It's so peaceful out here." Thomas took a deep breath of the mountain air as some of the years of built-up tension glided away.

The train car rocked a little, and Brandon lightly bumped him. He turned, and their gazes met once again. Brandon blinked, his thick lashes framing his incredible blue eyes. "Yes, it is. It's like job searches and appointments, meetings, and all that other stuff doesn't exist. At least for a little while."

"What kind of job were you hoping to get?" Thomas asked. "I know being an assistant wasn't your ultimate goal." He swallowed hard, realizing he was getting the benefit of someone as organized and capable as Brandon only until he found another job.

Brandon chuckled and turned to look out the window. The train traveled along the side of a mountain, the peak on one side and a ravine with the creek on the other. It was a stunning view, but Thomas barely noticed it as the sun caught Brandon's hair, setting it alight in an almost golden halo.

"I was hoping to get a job in the film or entertainment industry. Not as an actor or anything, but I have some experience—good experience, with results—and I was hoping it would get me noticed." Brandon shrugged, but Thomas could tell he was covering up for a disappointment that went deeper than he was letting on.

Thomas put his arm around Brandon's shoulder, and Brandon turned away from the view to look at him. Those eyes…. Thomas could get lost in those eyes, as big as the mountain sky and twice as beautiful. "You are going to find a great job, and someone is going to snatch you right away from me." He flashed a smile of his own even as his gut clenched slightly at the idea, but he had to be reasonable. "Sometimes it takes a little luck, but perseverance almost always pays off."

Brandon leaned against him for a second and then straightened up again. "Thanks, Thomas. I keep trying." He sighed and leaned forward, and Thomas let his touch slip away. If that wasn't welcome, Thomas certainly wasn't going to press. He'd probably stepped over the line anyway.

"Sorry," Thomas muttered and pulled his arm back, setting his hands in his lap.

Brandon flashed his blue eyes in his direction. "What for? It's me who should be sorry," he said softly. "I was leaning against you and…." Brandon's eyes grew heated for a second, and then his lips curled upward and his expression grew animated. He laughed quietly.

"I don't understand what's funny," Thomas grumped, then wished he hadn't.

"Us." Brandon's laughter died away. "You were apologizing for having your arm around me, and I was apologizing for leaning on you." He blinked, leaning a little closer. "And I liked both of them. They were nice." He sat back, and it was Thomas's turn to be confused, but only for a second, as Brandon once again leaned on him when the train began making a large loop through the old gold fields.

The recorded narration continued, but Thomas barely heard it, his attention riveted on everywhere Brandon touched him. His heart beat faster and he grew warmer by the second. He could simply move away and bring this gentle intimacy to an end that easily, but frankly he was afraid to move in case Brandon realized what he was doing. It felt so good—too good—being touched in such a simple way, rocking slightly along with the train as it made its way slowly along the tracks.

"Yes, they are." Thomas expected guilt and recrimination to creep in. They always did, especially if he thought of Angus, and he did… way too damn much. But not this time. Sure, he thought about his ex for, like, two seconds, and then joy, happiness, and contentment washed in. He deserved those and let things be for now.

The train ride took an hour, and once they were back at the station, Thomas didn't want to move. The others filed out, talking and laughing, rehashing the trip and what they liked best. Neither he nor Brandon moved for a full minute, and then Thomas slowly got to his feet, the fantasy over. He blinked and walked down the aisle, letting Brandon go first. They stepped off the train and out to the exit. People laughed and talked, scampering around him, and Thomas stood in the middle of the path, not moving.

"Thomas," Brandon said as he tugged lightly at his arm. "We need to get out of the way."

Thomas nodded and made his way down to the sidewalk. "Have you ever been in the middle of a crowd of people and felt utterly alone?" he asked just above a whisper.

"Yes. Definitely. Most of high school. I have friends and my grandma. My mom and dad aren't part of my life very much. They don't accept the fact that I'm gay, and refuse to have much to do with me. I don't fit in with parts of my own family." Brandon shrugged. "I know moving to a new place is hard, but you'll meet people. It will happen. It just takes time. Ask your mom and dad. They know everybody, it seems." Brandon smiled, but Thomas shook his head.

"That isn't it. I have friends in New York, but I can still stand in a room there and be completely alone. I'm the boss—I see hundreds of people a day, and yet it's mostly just business. We meet, come to an agreement, and they go back to their lives and I go home."

"I'm sure that's not true. You said you have friends. So call them and talk to them," Brandon offered, and Thomas knew he wasn't making himself plain. It wasn't his friends or his business associates or even his parents that were the problem; it was him.

"There's nothing they can do for me." Thomas took a few more steps, then realized he'd already said way too much to someone he'd only met two days ago but already felt like he could say just about anything to. "God, I'm going crazy."

"No, you aren't," Brandon said from behind him, and Thomas whirled around, not realizing he'd said that out loud. Brandon walked up to him. "You're trying to find a new direction in your life, and that's not easy for anyone." He took Thomas's hand right there on the street. "Finding a new way takes a leap of faith and some of that perseverance you were talking about before."

Thomas coughed, his throat dry. Dammit, how had Brandon gotten so damn smart and observant? "It's a pain in the ass is what it is. I had a life I understood that was reasonably predictable in its own way. I was calling the shots, controlling things in my life."

Brandon started down the street, and Thomas walked after him. "So? Things are different now. This isn't New York. It's Colorado Springs. People here are different, but I think you'll find they're a whole lot easier to get to know."

"Okay," Thomas agreed. That was probably true. "But I'm not talking about that."

Brandon stopped on the sidewalk. "I know what you're talking about. You of all people should know that you can do any damn thing you put your mind to.

You built buildings in New York, for God's sake. You can do anything you want to do."

Anything except shake the loneliness that had been with him for a long time. Thomas had just ignored it and gone on working, and now, after making this move, he had more time and couldn't ignore it anymore. "That's enough of this." This topic was only adding to his depression, and he'd come here hoping for some fun. He led the way down the street. "We're here, so let's have some fun."

"We could go down in the mine," Brandon offered. "They have one where you can go a thousand feet underground and see the gold veins and stuff like that. It's supposed to be pretty cool."

"You've never done it?" Thomas asked.

Brandon paused. "Nope. We were supposed to do it when I was in school, but I hate enclosed spaces, so I asked my mom to send me a note and one of the teachers had to wait up top with me."

"If you don't like enclosed spaces, then why offer to go?"

Brandon shrugged. "I didn't want you to be disappointed if that was something you really wanted to do."

Thomas rolled his eyes. "Come on. Let's be real tourists and see what souvenirs they have. We can buy a bunch of crap and send it back to Marjorie and Blaze. They'll think I've gone off my nut." He found he liked that idea.

Brandon laughed. "What does Marjorie like? Does she collect anything?"

Thomas shook his head. "Nope. She's a pretty no-frills, uncluttered kind of lady. At Christmas she brings in a small Christmas tree that she sets on one of the filing cabinets. That's the only decoration she brings in of any kind. She's amazing, don't get me wrong, but in New York, space is a premium so...." He shrugged.

"Okay. Then how about we try to find the tackiest souvenir possible to send to her?" Brandon's suggestion made Thomas grin.

"Awesome. We can each send her one and see which she complains about most." That left them both cackling as they headed into the first shop.

The lady behind the counter turned to them both as they giggled their way into the shop. Thomas passed the samples of gold-bearing quartz and bottles with gold flakes to go to the racks of souvenirs.

"What on earth is this?" Brandon whispered and held up a dolphin bottle opener that said Cripple Creek on it.

Thomas laughed and held his side. "What does a dolphin in the water have to do with Cripple Creek? We're at seven thousand feet." He shook his head. "That's definitely a contender."

"Yup." Brandon held on to the opener and continued looking. "Or maybe this?" It was a glass in the shape of a hunk of stone. "A rocks glass?" he quipped, and Thomas's chuckle returned.

The lady behind the counter turned to give them both dirty looks.

In the end Brandon bought the rocks glass, and Thomas left with a package of bacon bandages.

"I don't get it," Brandon said when Thomas showed them to him.

"Marjorie is vegetarian, but she loves bacon. She has been largely vegetarian for as long as I've known her, but she eats bacon because she can't bear to give it up." Thomas tossed the package in the air and caught it. "What's next?"

"Food?" Brandon suggested.

They'd eaten the snacks Brandon had packed in his pockets while they were on the train, and Thomas was starting to get hungry. They went into one of the saloons and sat down at the rough table. The server, wearing period garb, brought menus, and they ordered some nachos, which came served on a tin plate.

"They really need help with their authenticity," Brandon whispered.

"Yeah, but can you imagine what the food would be? Beans, beans, beans, and jerky. That would be a really interesting menu." Thomas was kidding, but it made Brandon smile again. He could become addicted to those smiles and would work to see them more often.

They ate, and drank plenty of water, which Thomas needed to remember to do until he got used to the altitude. Thomas paid the bill when it was presented.

"What else?" Brandon sat back in his chair. "Authentic or not, they were good."

"Do you feel lucky?" Thomas asked, turning to the casino across the street. "We could see what Lady Luck has in store."

"I don't know how to play any of the games, and slots are a real waste of money." Brandon shrugged. "I never had the inclination to play."

"I'll teach you. There are games that require skill as well as luck." Thomas started across the street and into the Double Eagle Casino. He looked around. It was small compared to Vegas, with a number of slots and a few tables. "We can try our luck at blackjack. We don't need to spend a lot."

Brandon clearly wasn't so sure, but Thomas ambled up to one of the tables with two empty seats. He pulled out a hundred and got chips, then passed half of them to Brandon. "Just have fun."

"You sure?" Brandon asked.

"Yeah." Thomas shrugged and placed a ten-dollar bet. Brandon bet five, and the dealer dealt the cards.

"Blackjack," the dealer said when Brandon got an ace and king. He was paid, and they continued playing.

Thomas lost and placed another bet. This time the dealer went bust and both of them won. The next few hands were pretty abysmal, and they lost, their stacks dwindling.

"Maybe we should go?" Brandon offered, and Thomas nodded. He bet everything on the last hand and got a blackjack. Brandon won as well, and when they gathered the chips, they were five bucks ahead. Thomas cashed them in before they left the casino.

"Did you have a good time?"

"It was fun. But I always had to work too hard for my money to be able to gamble with it. I know it sounds dumb, and if you look on it as entertainment and are careful, it can be fun. But I was always too worried about losing what I had, so I never played."

They continued down the sidewalk, passing a candy store that smelled heavenly of chocolate. Thomas veered inside and inhaled the delectable scent, his mouth watering. "I have a weakness…," he confessed to Brandon. "Chocolate is like my kryptonite. I don't have it in the house much because I'll sit down and eat it all at once." As he drooled over the chocolate case, Brandon pointed to a bag of caramel corn.

"This is mine," Brandon said, and Thomas grinned as he placed a large bag of caramel corn on the counter and got some mint meltaways and coconut clusters. He paid for all the naughtiness, and they left the store. It was getting late in the day, and they decided it was time to head back.

"I hate times like this."

"What?" Thomas asked.

"This was a lot of fun and I had a great time. But now it's over and time to go back to work." Brandon sighed. "Thank you for a fun day. I really appreciate it."

They reached the car and got inside. Thomas started the engine and turned to make sure Brandon's seat belt was fastened. Brandon looked back at him, his eyes once again filled with heat, which vanished within seconds. Thomas didn't look away, half daring Brandon to do the same. The inside of the car grew stuffy and warm. Thomas tugged at his collar to alleviate some of the heat, even as the air-conditioning kicked on full. This game was becoming a little much, but Thomas ignored the tension and eventually blinked away the connection to put the car into reverse and back out of the parking spot.

"THANK YOU for taking me today. That was fun and something you didn't need to do. I mean, I don't think you're paying me to be a tourist." Brandon unlocked the house and went inside. Thomas followed him into the kitchen just in time to see Brandon snatch up his list of tasks. "It was a lot of fun." Brandon scanned his list, and Thomas studied him, leaning on the counter. "What?"

"Nothing. I was just watching you."

Brandon snorted softly. "You do that a lot."

Thomas widened his eyes. Man, Brandon said what was on his mind. "I should go upstairs and change clothes." Maybe he should disappear for a while. Brandon would certainly leave soon and give him a chance to breathe again.

"I still have a few errands to run for you." Brandon left the room, and the *thunk* of the washer and dryer doors opening and closing reached Thomas's ears, followed by the hum of the dryer. Then Brandon returned. "I need to get you some things or you're going to be left high and dry in the bathroom." He winked, and Thomas nodded. Obviously Brandon was all business, and that's what he should be as well. "Look, today was great, but I know this was a one-off kind of thing. It was still a lot of fun, and I can't wait to send our stuff to Marjorie." He chuckled, and Thomas did the same, remembering the fun in the store.

It had been a long time since he'd laughed like that. Oh, he had fun sometimes, but not belly-laugh, let-it-all-go-and-just-be-yourself fun. That he'd have to scour his memory for, it had been so long. "Yes, it was. Today was kind of special." He pushed away from the counter, then froze as Brandon caught his gaze, holding it. Thomas had imagined what Brandon's lips would taste like for days, and he wondered if he was about to find out.

Thomas was afraid to move. If he did, he might chicken out. On the other hand, if he leaned forward,

Brandon might do the same and then they'd be kissing, which could lead to Thomas finding out the answers to all those questions that he'd been asking himself every time he caught a glimpse of what was under Brandon's shirt.

Hell, he shouldn't be having these thoughts at all. Brandon worked for him, and Thomas should keep a professional distance, but that was hard when they'd just spent the day having a blast together. That, too, was his fault. He should have known better. He let himself get sucked in by Brandon's blue eyes, and those full lips that just begged to be kissed. Thomas blinked, and Brandon seemed to have moved closer. Thomas held his breath and took a single small step forward, hoping Brandon would do the same.

He did. They were inches apart, and the dryer and every other sound in the house quieted, except for the beating of his heart in his ears. If he were honest, he wanted this.

Thomas's reservations flew out the window and he started closing the distance between them.

His phone rang, chiming in his pocket. Thomas tried to ignore it, but Brandon had already pulled away. Thomas yanked his phone out of his pocket, huffing at Marjorie's name on the screen. "I'd better take this," he half growled.

Brandon nodded and turned away. "I'll see you in the morning," he said softly, and hurried out of the room.

Thomas sighed under his breath as he took the call, wishing her timing had been better. So much better.

Chapter 6

BRANDON STOOD outside the front door to Thomas's house the next morning, bags of toilet paper and other things in his hand. He was nervous and had been up for most of the night. Thomas had come close to kissing him. Brandon was pretty sure of that because he'd been equally close to kissing Thomas. Thomas liked him and was attracted the same way Brandon was, which was cool because he liked that Thomas liked him. Okay, his head was going around in circles until he sounded like an angsty teenager.

Yeah, he'd have liked it if Thomas had kissed him, but that damn phone call.... And then Brandon had the chance to realize how ridiculous that idea was. Thomas was übersuccessful, and Brandon was his assistant, stopping on the way home to buy his toilet paper. It didn't matter that just the thought of Thomas kissing him sent his heart racing, or the fact that he had been up half the night with his imagination running completely wild. Now Brandon was nervous and unsure how to act. He figured the best thing to do was to pretend the whole thing had never happened. That way Thomas could go on and Brandon could simply go back to work like normal.

He unlocked the door and went quietly into the house. Brandon put the bags on the counter, then went to the laundry room, where he pulled the towels out of the dryer and folded them. He left them on top, figuring he could put them away once Thomas was awake.

Brandon checked what was in the refrigerator, then set up the coffeepot and got it brewing, the scent filling the room. If he were correct, that would most likely draw Thomas out of his room like a cartoon character.

The doorbell sounded as the coffee finished, and Brandon answered it. "Good morning," Brandon said, and ushered the representative from the maid service into the family room. "I'm Brandon, Mr. Stepford's assistant."

"Helen Gracos." They shook hands, and Brandon offered her a seat. Helen seemed very efficient and got right down to business. "What sort of work is Mr. Stepford looking for?"

"Well, probably two times a week to do the cleaning, laundry, and things like that. The house is quite large, but there are rooms that aren't being used at the moment."

"I see. Will there be any shopping required?" she asked, making notes in a small book.

"No. I'll be taking care of most of that. You'll be cleaning and taking care of the laundry. The things

he sends out to the cleaners, I'll be in charge of."
It seemed very straightforward to him, and Helen
seemed pleased.

"We'd be happy to add Mr. Stepford to our cli-
ents." She looked around and made a few more notes.
"I'll send over an agreement that states our duties and
rates. It seems to me that once a week or so might suffice." She hummed softly to herself as she thought. "A
single person in a house like this shouldn't make much
mess, but we can start with twice a week and make
adjustments. We might do a heavier cleaning once a
week and something lighter on the second day."

"That's great. While Thomas is only renting this
house, my impression is that he'll be looking for a permanent residence in the area. So hopefully this isn't
a short-term contract." At least he thought so. It had
occurred to him that, after the lease was up, Thomas might just return to New York, though he hoped
Thomas was able to make a good life for himself here.

She nodded. "I understand. Like I said, I'll send
over an agreement. I feel it's best if both parties clearly know and understand what's expected. Please have
him look it over, and if he agrees, we can get started."
She stood, and they shook hands once again. Then
Brandon showed Helen out and went into the kitchen.

He had a cup of coffee, put the things he'd bought
away, and then checked the clock. It was after nine.
He remembered seeing Thomas's car in the drive, so
he assumed he was home, but Thomas was usually up
by now. Even the day of his hangover, he'd been up
by this time.

Quietly, Brandon went upstairs. Thomas's door
was closed, and he knocked softly. When he didn't

receive an answer, he cracked the door. "Thomas...,"
he said softly, wrinkling his nose at the stale air that
wafted out. "Are you all right?"

"Yes," Thomas groaned.

"You have a call in half an hour. Do you want me
to bring you anything?" He kept his voice low, sus-
pecting that Thomas had once again been out drinking.

"Is there coffee?" he mumbled.

"Yes. It's already made. There's aspirin in the
medicine cabinet if you need them, and I can bring
you some water or...."

"No." Thomas slowly sat up, the covers falling
away from his chest. "I'm okay. Just stupid." He
blinked and stood, revealing only a pair of plaid box-
ers clinging to his hips.

Brandon backed out of the room and closed the
door once again. He headed back downstairs and went
into the office to make sure the computer and everything was set up for the meeting. He didn't really need
to, but Brandon needed to do *something*.

He called Marjorie and went over the schedule
for the day. There were two meetings, and Brandon
used Thomas's laptop to bring up his calendar. Marjorie also sent him a number of documents that Brandon
was going to need to get printed. He figured he should
talk to Thomas about buying and setting up a printer
for his office.

Brandon got the files together on a flash drive
and slipped it into his pocket so he could take them to
the printshop. As he finished, he heard Thomas in the
kitchen and joined him there.

Thomas looked like he'd just been over fifty miles
of bad road. Brandon wanted to ask what he'd done

and why, but he held his tongue. It was none of his business. But damn, the way Thomas sat at the counter, staring at his mug, the appliances—at anything and anywhere but looking at him—was rather creepy.

"I have some files I need to have printed for you, and I was wondering if you wanted me to get you a printer for your office."

"I'll order one and have it delivered," Thomas said flatly. God, what a difference from the happy, laughing guy from the afternoon before. "Just go get that stuff printed for me. I'll be in my meeting, so be quiet when you get back." With that pronouncement, he left the room, taking his coffee with him.

"Yes, your majesty," Brandon said under his breath, wondering if yesterday had been a fluke and the Thomas he was seeing today was the real guy. Brandon wasn't sure, but the jerk who'd just left the room wasn't very endearing… at all.

Still, he had a job to do, so he hurried to the local printshop, made a single copy of each of the documents, and returned. The office door was closed, but he cracked it, set the papers on the desk, and left again quickly.

Thomas barely looked up from his call.

Brandon wondered about calling Marjorie to find out if Thomas was a mood swing kind of guy, but he didn't think so, contrary to the evidence in front of him. Rather, Brandon got the distinct feeling that this was specially directed at him. When he'd overheard Thomas on the phone, he had sounded upbeat, cheerful, almost happy. Shit, if he'd done something wrong….

"Brandon," Thomas called, not sounding happy now, and Brandon found him in his office doorway. "I need you to call Marjorie and tell her to get Blaze in my office and on this call... now." He stepped back and closed the door.

Brandon made the call.

"Brandon," Marjorie said when she answered. At least someone was happy to talk to him today.

"Thomas said to call and have you get Blaze on the call he's on right away. He was pretty upset and snippy."

"Okay, I'm on it. Message Thomas and tell him I'm running Blaze down." She hung up, and Brandon sent the message, then put the laundry away and took care of the other things around the house.

After an hour, Thomas came out of the office, wiping his forehead with a tissue. "Thank you."

"Get the problem handled?" Brandon asked.

"Yeah. We saved an entire deal and six months of work from falling apart." Thomas let his hand fall to his side with a sigh.

"Did they want more money?"

Thomas shook his head. "Not everything is about money. There's a piece of open land behind the development site that's part of the deal that the community has been using as a garden. The owner wanted it to remain that way and was very concerned about that. But we needed that land in order to make the development pay off. Blaze pointed out that we owned a small lot a half block away. We had planned to build an apartment building on it, but that project was on hold. So we agreed to move the garden there. Everyone was happy."

"That's pretty cool," Brandon said. "You get what you want and help the community at the same time." Brandon figured green space in New York was always a premium and pretty special.

"Yeah. Though we will retain ownership of the property. When we looked at the community garden, it didn't seem active, so we did agree to revisit the community garden based on how much it's used." Thomas sighed. "God, I need coffee."

"How about some breakfast?" Brandon offered, and Thomas groaned. "I know I'm only your assistant, but you wouldn't feel like shit if you didn't drink so much." He frowned and went into the kitchen to grab the trash container, which jingled with glass bottles, and took it out to recycle. He sighed. It truly was none of his business if Thomas wanted to drink.

"There wouldn't be a problem if you weren't here," Thomas groused.

"Then why did you hire me?" Brandon dropped the liner back in the trash can. God, the guy was a dickhead today.

"Because you were the best for the job, but I keep thinking about you all the damn time." Thomas rubbed the back of his neck. "I should go back to work."

"Sure, hide behind work rather than say what you mean," Brandon snapped and immediately wished he'd kept his mouth shut. It wasn't good that he was having an argument with his boss. Thomas turned, his eyes swirling with confusion, and Brandon decided his only course of action was to push forward. "Yesterday you were nice, and today you're snappy and telling me I'm a problem. What do you want, Thomas?"

"You're not the one with the problem. I am."
Thomas rubbed his temples. "I can't seem to get you
out of my head, and you shouldn't be there—you
work for me. I can't figure shit out."

Brandon frowned. "So? Imagine having you in
my head since I was fifteen and see how easy shit is."

Thomas stood stock-still. "Fifteen…," he whispered. "Why? How?"

"You don't remember, do you? I mowed your
lawn that year before you left and went to New York.
I knocked on your door, and you opened it and made
my little gay fifteen-year-old heart practically stop
beating. You were in a pair of jeans and no shirt. You
looked… damn… and I stood there, trying to form
words in front of the hunk of the year."

"Shit…. And you remembered that?" Thomas
grew quiet. "I don't at all."

"Of course you don't. I was some kid who came to
mow your lawn, and you answered the door without a
shirt because you were probably busy. You made a deal,
and I got to work. I suspect you never gave me a second
thought except to pay me for what I did for you."

Thomas shook his head slowly. "And you've remembered that all this time?" He seemed shocked,
and Brandon figured he had a right to be.

"Not sharply, I guess, but…." He wasn't going
to say that Thomas had fired his teenage imagination
for the longest time after that day. It was embarrassing
and would probably make Thomas more uncomfortable than he already was.

"'The hunk of the year'?" Thomas asked, and
Brandon felt his cheeks warm. Then Thomas chuckled. "Man, someday you're going to have to tell me

more about that. I haven't felt like a hunk-of-the-year type of guy in a very long time." He seemed pleased about that idea.

"Have you not looked in the mirror lately?" Brandon asked.

"Yeah. I know what I look like. I'm a man who works too damn much and is approaching forty in a matter of weeks." Thomas sighed again. That was becoming some kind of nervous habit or something. "I'm…."

"I know what you are and how old you are. What does that have to do with anything?" Brandon put his hands on his hips. "That doesn't explain the grumpbucket you've been all day."

"I almost kissed you yesterday." Thomas said the words as though they explained everything.

"So? I almost kissed *you*, and then you pulled away with that stupid phone call, and I got cold feet." Brandon shifted his weight from foot to foot. "I'm not saying that we need to do anything. If you aren't interested or don't want to do anything with me—"

Thomas leaned against the wall. "God. It isn't like I don't want you…. At night I can't sleep because I keep seeing your eyes, and when I do sleep, you're in my head and I have very vivid dreams. I got up last night and drank the beer in the refrigerator to try to get numb enough that I could get back to sleep." Thomas put up his hands when Brandon moved closer. "This is all my fault. I've had a history of having… feelings for the people I work with, and it turned out really badly."

Brandon took a step back. "Okay. I can understand that." He turned to leave the room. There was no reason to pursue this. He was an adult, and he and

Thomas had at least spoken about what was going on. In a way, that made things better because there wasn't all this silent attraction going on with neither of them talking about it.

"Brandon," Thomas said from behind him, the timbre of his voice low and deep, resonating in Brandon's gut. He turned, and Thomas cupped his cheeks, kissing him with enough energy to short-circuit Brandon's brain.

He took a single step back, the wall stopping his momentary retreat and providing support as Brandon ran his hands up Thomas's arms to his body, using him as a road map, because his entire attention was centered on the point where Thomas's lips touched his. He'd imagined how this would feel since he was fifteen, and damn it all, reality made his dreams pale by comparison. Maybe there was something wrong with his imagination or....

Fuck it all, he was worried about his imagination when the object of said imaginings had him pressed to the wall and was kissing him to within an inch of his life. Brandon let go of all other thoughts and kissed Thomas back, holding him tight until he couldn't breathe any longer. Brandon broke away, looking into Thomas's deep and dreamy eyes, long enough to catch a breath of air, and then, desperately afraid Thomas was going to back away, kissed him again with even more intensity. Thomas shook in his arms, and Brandon cupped his head, feasting on Thomas's lips, tongue slipping between his, getting a good taste of his maleness.

When Brandon pulled away, Thomas did too, and they stared at each other. Thomas blinked and sighed first, and Brandon did the same, and then they both smiled and began to laugh.

"God, I've wanted that since I was fifteen."

"I may not have imagined kissing you for all that time, but I've wanted something like that my whole life." Thomas gasped, his chest heaving.

A knock on the front door made them jump apart. Thomas headed out front, while Brandon checked his list to make sure he hadn't missed an appointment.

"Hey, Mom," Thomas said, and Brandon breathed a quick sigh of relief that he hadn't forgotten anything.

"I thought I'd come by and make sure you weren't working all the time." Mrs. Stepford sniffed as Brandon entered the hall. "Drinking again?" She wrinkled her nose, and Brandon turned away. "You can smell that sort of thing. It leaks out of your pores, and no nice boy is going to want a drunk for a husband." She continued on inside as Thomas closed the door, rolling his eyes. "Brandon, how's your grandmother?" Mrs. Stepford stopped in front of him, patting his cheek. "Now, don't you let this son of mine work you too hard. He gets caught up in whatever he's doing and forgets everything, including his manners sometimes."

"Mom, things are going well."

Mrs. Stepford looked at both of them and smiled knowingly. Brandon wondered if she'd been peering in the windows and seen them kissing, but that wasn't likely, and Mrs. Stepford wasn't going to go rummaging through the bushes in front of her son's house. That was the stupidest idea on earth. Still, the way she looked at him made Brandon feel exposed... or guilty. He wasn't sure which—maybe a little of both?

"I made you some potato salad and chicken salad. They're in the car."

"I'll go get them," Brandon offered and hurried out the door. That would at least give him a few seconds so when he returned, things could look like normal, and besides, he was Thomas's assistant. He needed to act like it.

Damn, he needed to get his head in the game and out of his pants.

Brandon opened the back door and pulled out the cardboard box stacked with at least six bowls. He brought it inside, checked out each one, and slid them into the refrigerator. At least Thomas wasn't going to starve, and he'd have some good home cooking.

"I was thinking that you should join a couple of the local business groups," Mrs. Stepford was saying. "They've been talking about revitalizing the downtown area to make it more appealing and vibrant instead of just relying on tourist shops and stuff. I bet you could help with that."

"Mom, I'm fine...."

"No, you're not. I know you," she was saying, and Brandon stayed out of the family room, deciding to use Thomas's office as a quiet space to check Thomas's schedule.

Brandon reviewed all his emails and touched base with Marjorie, who complimented him on his quick action from that morning.

"I have some paperwork and personal papers that have come to the office for him. I'm overnighting them to the house there."

"I'll look for them." Brandon made a note. "I haven't received the phone and tablet."

"They should come tomorrow." She typed in the background, and Brandon made more notes.

"Thanks. I spoke to Thomas about a printer for the office, and he said he'd order one. But I don't think he'll remember, and he needs one. I can get it set up for him."

"I'll have the IT department order and send one to the house. That way if there are any troubles, he can have it supported through them." The typing became more intense for a few seconds. "There. I copied Thomas on the request so he'll know it's done. Is there anything else?"

"I need some more to do," Brandon said. "I mean, I know I'm his assistant, but I can't just stand around here and wait for him to need something. He isn't that needy or messy, and…."

"Very good. Let me give it some thought. The end of the month is coming up, and that means endless reports for him to review and the email volume goes through the roof. I should send you a laptop as well so you have something proper to work on. I'll see if we can get one sent right away." Marjorie seemed to think of everything. "I have another call. But let me know when the equipment and the envelope arrive."

"I will," Brandon promised, and ended the call. He left the office and peered into the family room, where Mrs. Stepford continued talking full steam, barely pausing for breath. Thomas looked trapped, and Brandon had to try to help. "Excuse me. Thomas, I need to remind you about your call in five minutes."

Thomas turned to him, blinking as though wondering what Brandon was talking about. Then his eyes widened. "Oh y-yes," he stammered. He turned back to his mother. "I really need to prepare. You're welcome to stay here if you'd like."

"I'm expecting the museum people this afternoon to hang the paintings. I'll bring your lunch into the office for you in a little while."

Thomas gave him a grateful look, then kissed his mom and scampered off into his office, closing the door.

"Do you want some lunch?" Brandon asked Mrs. Stepford. He'd known her almost all of his life, as she and his grandma were best friends. "We have plenty now." They shared a smile.

"I have to get home and make Harold his lunch. He's been out working in the yard." She stood and patted his cheek. "You're a good boy. You always have been, and your grandmother is so proud of you."

Brandon nodded, giving her a smile.

"Do you hear from your mom and dad?"

"Not much. They don't agree with some of my 'life choices' and…." He sighed. "They have other kids, so I guess I didn't matter so much." He didn't want that to be true, but it was how he felt.

Mrs. Stepford patted his hand. "I never understood your father or how he could be related to Thelma. She doesn't have a judgmental bone in her body and accepts everyone for who they are."

Brandon shrugged. "I'd like to be able to say that my mother would accept me, but that would be a lie. My father makes no secret of how he feels either." He smiled. "I gotta give Grandma credit—she doesn't take any of his crap and tells him he's a dang fool every chance she gets." Unfortunately his brother and sister seemed to feel the same way his parents did, because neither of them was calling to see how he was doing. There was nothing he could do about any of it.

"Well, you make yourself happy. That's all we can really do. And I'll tell you what a friend of Thomas's told me once, years ago." She smiled and squeezed his hand. "Have you met Blaze?"

Brandon shook his head.

"Well, he and Thomas were college roommates, and he told me once, after Thomas came out, that sometimes gay people—hell, all of us—we have the family we're born into, and then there's the one we make. So the family you were born into was crap... well, most of it." She rolled her eyes dramatically. "You just set out to make your own." Mrs. Stepford leaned closer. "And don't look so hard that you over-look what's right in front of you." She winked, stand-ing and slowly making her way toward the front door. As she passed Thomas's office, she opened the door and stuck her head in. "Don't you think for a second that I don't know you've been hiding in here." She clicked her tongue. "Shame on you trying to get away from your mother who loves you."

"I just finished up my call." Thomas joined her and walked her out, so Brandon went into the kitch-en to get some lunch together. "Thanks for the inter-ference," Thomas said when he returned. "I love my mom dearly, but she can be pretty strident, especially when she's on one of her matchmaking pushes."

"Oh man...," Brandon said as he put some bread in the toaster to go with the chicken salad. At least that explained some of what Mrs. Stepford had said to him.

"Yeah. She has never been successful as far as I know. My mom introduced my brother to his first wife, Karla. The entire family stopped speaking to both of them because of that woman. I actually brought it up to her—thought that would buy me some time. Nope." Thomas laughed. "You saved me from her setting me up with every gay man nearing forty in town. All four of them."

The toast popped, and Brandon got the plates together. He made sure Thomas was set and made a small plate for himself.

"I think I owe you an explanation... of sorts," Thomas began as he took his first bite. "Now, this brings me back. Mom has made this recipe for years." He ate a few bites and set his fork down.

"You don't owe me anything... not really. We've known each other for, like, three days, and other than me knowing what kind of toilet paper you prefer, we don't know anything about each other. So we can take things slow... if you want to take them at all. But there are a few rules."

"Okay." Thomas had an amused look on his face. "Since I'm usually the boss, I'm normally the one making the rules." He crossed his arms over his chest. "Go ahead."

"Well, during work hours, we're professional. I am your assistant, and even though we work at your house, during the day, this is a work environment. You're paying me to do a job, and I'm going to do that to the very best of my ability. No matter what. I don't know if anything is going to happen between us... though that kiss was more than promising." Brandon's lips still tingled from it.

"It seems like you've been giving this some thought," Thomas said.

"Well, I don't want to be paid for sex… and having sex on the job is kind of tacky." Brandon grinned. "I mean, you see it in these movies, and it always comes out as being a dumb thing to do, so why bother?" He bumped Thomas's shoulder. "Besides, do you want your mother coming in here, finding you bareassed in your office with—" Brandon didn't dare go on for multiple reasons, the first being the abject horror on Thomas's face and the way he shivered as Brandon went on. Plus, if he did, Brandon was going to start to blush, and he was getting a little tired of doing that all the dang time.

"Enough said." Thomas rolled his eyes and leaned closer to him. "But it's lunchtime now." Thomas lightly touched his chin, and Brandon turned just far enough that Thomas angled his face to kiss him. The creaminess and seasoning of the dressing added to the richness of Thomas as the kiss deepened. Brandon blindly set down his fork, hoping he didn't make too much of a mess while at the same time not really caring if he did. He could clean it up. His hands itched to touch, and he wound his arms around Thomas's neck, deepening the kiss that felt so right.

Suddenly he wasn't hungry anymore, at least for food. Thomas tasted better than anything else, and Brandon ached to get more of him. But he'd set the rules, and he was going to abide by them—not that it was going to be easy with Thomas's hunkiness around him all day. Brandon pulled back, slipping his arms and hands away. Now that he knew Thomas was interested in him, it was going to be difficult to keep his distance, but he had to... for now.

"Go ahead and eat your lunch," Brandon mock-scolded, then took a deep breath to try to cool his head and tamp down the urge to jump Thomas right there.

"Take things slow, huh," Thomas said breathily.

Brandon nodded. "Yeah, slow." How in the hell he'd do that, Brandon wasn't sure, but he'd been the one to propose it, mostly because he thought that was what Thomas would want.

"Somehow I don't think you take very many things slowly," Thomas quipped, and Brandon narrowed his gaze.

"What a mean thing to say," Brandon said before he could stop his mouth from engaging. "My dad used to tell me that I did things too fast all the time. Slow down, take your time, do it right." He'd heard it to the point that it really bothered him now. It was, in his mind, a precursor to being told he was doing something wrong.

"Excuse me?" Thomas said, bewildered. "You're always incredibly efficient, and so far you get things done faster and better than I would have expected. So why is that mean?"

Brandon turned away, embarrassed that he'd jumped to the wrong conclusion. "I try to get things done right the first time. That gets things done quicker because they don't need to be redone." He really didn't want to go into the dynamics of growing up with his impatient, self-righteous father.

"I wasn't being insulting in any way. It's just that you have energy and you throw yourself into what you do." Thomas returned to his lunch, and Brandon wished he'd kept his mouth shut. Now he felt the need to explain.

"Do you remember my parents, or did you know them?" Brandon asked. They were roughly Thomas's age, though a decade or so older.

"I think I met them when I was younger a couple of times. Your mom was a beautiful lady, as I remember."

"Yeah, and my father was hit with an ugly stick," Brandon groused.

Thomas leaned back, giving him a "what are you talking about?" look.

"On the inside."

"I see," Thomas said.

Brandon shook his head. "How could you?" He sighed. "Okay… in school we learned that there are three things to any talk: what you want, when you want it, and how to do it. My dad always wanted everything done exactly how he wanted it, when he wanted it done, and he never wanted to do it himself, so nothing was ever right. It made me nervous, so I'd try to do things faster so I could have time to change what he didn't like. It really sucked. I wasn't the son he wanted me to be, and I didn't become a doctor the way he wanted. And then I had the audacity to tell him I was gay, so he turned his back on me—something my grandma has never forgiven him for and I doubt she ever will." Thank God for her. It helped keep him sane when all hell had broken loose.

"Your father is a dentist, right?"

"Yeah. He reminds me of the one from *Little Shop of Horrors*. I swear, the man loves inflicting pain any way he fucking can." Brandon returned his attention to his lunch, attacking the food because he needed to do something with his energy. He hated talking about his father and wished he'd just go away.

"I didn't mean to push any of your buttons."

Brandon put down his fork again, feeling like shit. "I know. I shouldn't have brought it up." This whole thing with his family hurt him more than he wanted to admit. His mom and dad should love him uncon-ditionally, and instead they made him feel like he was never good enough and didn't live up to their ridicu-lous standards. "All my dad cares about is how things look for him, or his practice, and how they affect him. To hell with everyone else." Brandon took his dish-es to the sink and loaded them into the dishwasher. He sighed, not looking at Thomas. "I shouldn't have brought any of this up. It wasn't professional, and that's primarily what I'm here to do. This is work time, and I shouldn't be unloading my family crap on you." Brandon was here to help Thomas, not add to his issues or ask him to help. Brandon's parents were Brandon's problem, not Thomas's.

Brandon finished putting away the dishes and then closed the containers to set the rest of the food back in the refrigerator. He stopped when Thomas's hands settled on his shoulders.

"You have nothing to be sorry for. In New York I worked in an office with dozens of people, and each one of them looked out for me. They did what I want-ed them to do, and they all watched me for anything they thought I might need. I knew all their names, but for most of them, that was about it. I kept my distance. And I really didn't know any of them other than Blaze and Marjorie. It was a lonely, isolating life. I worked, I expected them to work, and when the pressure got too much and my body rebelled, the doctors said I needed to reduce stress, find a simpler life. I moved here, and if left to my own devices, I probably would have fallen into my old pattern all over again."

"O-kay." Brandon really wasn't sure what Thomas was trying to tell him.

"You have nothing to be ashamed of with talking about your family. You know enough about mine. I suspect my mother made sure of that."

Brandon chuckled. "She's a force of nature."

"Always was. There were times I think the wind stopped blowing simply because it was what she wanted." Thomas sighed. "I need to get back to work for a while. This project is more problematic than Blaze thinks it is. I have some cards and things that need to be mailed, and a list of supplies for the office."

Brandon nodded, and after taking care of the dishes, went to Thomas's office to get the list of what he needed. Then he left the house to get the errands done.

THAT EVENING, once Brandon had completed his work and had his list of tasks for the following day, he sat in the kitchen with a cup of coffee, going over everything, listening as Thomas moved about upstairs. He was about to go when Thomas's movements approached the top of the stairs. He descended, and Brandon paused as Thomas came into the kitchen.

"I need to get going for the night."

"Of course." Thomas seemed confused, and then walked over to him and engulfed Brandon in a hug before kissing him hard enough that the damn stool nearly toppled over backward. There was no doubt how Thomas was feeling at the moment, and the worries that had settled in for the afternoon sprouted wings and flew away. "I was thinking that on Saturday, if you don't have plans, we could go out to dinner. No work, no discussions of work, just a nice dinner."

"You mean, a date?" Brandon asked with a smile.

"Yes." Thomas leaned close, holding his hands at Brandon's shoulders. "I've had some time to think about it, and that's exactly what I mean. You've been working tentatively all day, tiptoeing around me like you don't know how I'm going to act, and I've been wondering how to behave without seeming like some lecherous old man."

"You aren't old—"

"I'm older than you, and I don't intend to make the same mistakes that I have in the past." Thomas swallowed hard. "So I'm asking you out to dinner and a movie or something on Saturday night. Neither of us will be working that day, and we can be just two people out together. Is that okay?" Thomas gave him an uncertain, hopeful look.

Brandon grinned. "That would be very nice."

A date, like a real date. Brandon wondered what a date with Thomas was going to be like and just how he was going to last until Saturday without getting so excited that he flew all to pieces.

Chapter 7

THE WEEK had gone well, and Thomas had done his best to take it easy and try not to stress over everything going on in the office. He spent a lot of time on the phone with Blaze. They worked through some procedures where Thomas would be involved with each project at certain steps to ensure they stayed on track or brought in if there were issues he could help with, but otherwise Blaze would take the lead as his senior project director and Thomas could step away a little from the day-to-day operations.

"I still want input on hiring and terminations." Thomas was adamant about that. He had put together a great team of people and wanted to keep it that way.

"Of course," Blaze said. "We'll also set up a Monday project overview and update meeting, as well as a Thursday project issues and resolution meeting to help you stay up to date."

"Great. But I don't want any dog and pony shows. If I get the feeling that these meetings are being stage-managed and prepared to the nth degree, I'll be on a plane to New York the following day to kick some ass." Thomas paused. "And you know where I'm going to start." Blaze might be his best friend, but as a senior executive with his company, Thomas held him to the highest business standards. And he knew how these things went.

"I agree," Blaze said, then grew quiet.

"What is it?" Thomas knew what the hesitation meant.

"The Swanson deal…," Blaze said. "I don't know what's going on, and it may be nothing, but it's been moving along perfectly and now there are questions. Nothing big, but… it's hard to put my finger on it. This could be me overreacting, and I'll tell you if anything comes of it right away. It's just my gut being a little titchy right now."

"Part of what I'm paying you for is your gut. Keep me informed."

THOMAS SPENT most of Saturday morning with his mom and dad, helping them with things around the house. His mom was slowing down, that was plain to see. She still cooked too much and worried about him too much, and when he'd taken her shopping, she'd forgotten her shopping list and had trouble remembering what was on it. Granted, that didn't indicate that anything was really wrong with her other than the fact that she was getting older, but he worried. In the end he'd called his dad, who had taken a picture of the list and sent it to him.

"Maybe I can see if Brandon would be willing to help you out? He's very organized, and he gets things done well."

His mother looked at him as though he were crazy. "I know you're busy and important and need assistants and things." She put her hands on her hips, stopping right in the middle of the canned goods aisle in the grocery store. "Brandon is a nice boy, but I don't want anyone in my business and doing my shopping for me." She shook her head. "I'm slowing down, not getting ready for the grave."

Thomas put his hands up. The last thing he wanted to do was fight. "I was just offering to see if he could help you. He goes to Costco for me, and he could see if you needed things when he goes."

She glared at him. "I'll think about it." She lowered her arms and turned, walking off down the aisle.

God, he could navigate extremely complicated real estate deals, and yet taking his mother to the grocery store had more pitfalls.

"Are you dating anyone?" she asked a few minutes later as another of those potholes opened up in front of him.

"No." That was technically true. He and Brandon were going out that evening, so they hadn't dated yet, so he wasn't dating anyone… at this exact moment. Yeah, he was being a shit, but he didn't want his mother butting into his private life.

"How is Collin? I talked to him for a few minutes earlier in the week, but we each got calls and had to cut it short." He smiled and his mother frowned. She knew he was getting at her for the whole Karla incident.

"Don't give me that sugar-sweet look." She turned around and continued on. "I'm your mother and I know you."

Thomas followed behind her. "You know, I came to see you to spend some time with you. Not go to the grocery store." It had probably been nearly a decade since he'd been in a store like this.

"We're spending time, aren't we, and you're helping me, so…?" She seemed particularly grouchy, and he saw her walking more slowly, favoring her right side. "Anyway, I want my sons to be happy—"

"Well, Collin is, now that he's free of Karla." Thomas knew he was turning the knife a little, but his mother needed to stay out of his love life. "Did you know that she kept him on an allowance? She controlled all the money and—"

"Yes, I know. She's trying to say that all the money in the accounts is hers. I helped your brother get a good attorney. She's amazing. I met her at a ladies' guild meeting at church." His mother stopped and turned to him, adding in a whisper, "She's a complete and total witch, always trying to foist her ideas on the rest of us, who rarely get a word in edgewise. So she's perfect to sic on Karla and will rip her to pieces." Mother continued her shopping, and Thomas did his best to help, but she just seemed to want company. "Do you think Brandon is lonely?" She put a couple cans of beans and corn in her cart. "He's really sweet, and there are some young men that I met at…." She tapped the arm of the cart. "Oh yeah, at the Toasted Bean, who were very nice and about his age."

"Mom. No matchmaking. Not for me, and not for any of the people who work for me." He was getting tired of this entire situation. "Just let it go. Everyone is perfectly capable of managing their own love life." He'd unintentionally raised his voice, and a couple of the other people in the aisle turned to him.

His mother scoffed and rolled her eyes before continuing. "Let's get this over with. I'm not getting any younger." She picked up speed, finished her shopping, and got in line at the checkouts. Thomas handed the cashier his credit card, and once the groceries were paid for, he carried them out to the car.

When they got home, she put the things away and Thomas went in search of his father. He found him in his small workshop in the shed in the backyard.

"Is this where you hide?" Thomas asked his dad as soon as the door closed. He sighed. "Mom needs more care than I'd realized. I suppose this is where you go when you need a few minutes."

"Yeah." Dad leaned against the counter with a small sigh, getting sawdust on his pants and shirt, before reaching down to open a hidden refrigerator. "Ready for a beer?"

"It's too early. I haven't even had lunch." Thomas was pleased when his dad pulled out a couple of Diet Cokes and once again leaned against the counter, handing him one before popping the top on the other. "What do you want to do while I'm here, Dad?"

"Who says we have to do anything?" His dad smiled and lifted a box to reveal a small television. "I have everything I could possibly want out here. I love your mother, but sometimes I just need a moment to myself." He pulled out a couple of chairs. "What's on your mind?" He sat down and looked at Thomas with interest.

"I came here to spend more time with you and Mom." He took the other chair. "I've been so wrapped up in myself and my work for so long that I think I lost track of what was really important." It was hard for Thomas to see his parents getting older, his mom's health fading, knowing he'd missed a lot of years with them and that he was only going to have so much time left before it was too late.

"What did you expect? The two of us spending our days in rocking chairs on the front porch? We keep busy, have friends, even do dinner parties sometimes. Your mom loves to cook. I swear sometimes it's what she lives for." Dad patted his belly. He had clearly been the beneficiary of that cooking for years.

"I don't know." Thomas sighed and drank some of his soda.

"I guess the changes are with you. Are you making friends and meeting people?"

"I have a date tonight," he confessed, and his father nodded, lightly scratching his gray head. "But I don't want Mom to know."

"Smart man. She'll get in the middle of it faster than you can say Dolly Levi." His father chuckled and then sighed. "It's about time you got over all that nonsense with Angus. He was a real shit."

"Dad!" His father never swore. Growing up, it had been his mother who could make a sailor blush, and where Thomas had learned every swear word known under creation. Lord, that woman could curse a blue streak.

"It's not a lie. He was a conniving little weasel, and I was glad when you kicked him to the curb. And the rest of it… well, things worked out in the end, but you gave us the scare of our lives." His dad set the can on the work counter, leaning forward. "Who is your date with?"

Thomas hesitated.

His father shook his head. "Getting involved with people you work with is a bad idea."

"I know. But it's Brandon, Thelma's grandson," Thomas confessed. "He's special, Dad. Brandon gets me and seems to understand what I need."

"Well, take things slow, for goodness' sake."

"That's what Brandon said." There was a good point in his corner. "So we're going on a date tonight. Like, out to dinner and then a movie. Old-fashioned stuff." Thomas caught his dad's gaze. "Believe it or not, I'm less concerned with Brandon doing anything at work, the way Angus did, than the fact that he's going to get an opportunity somewhere and leave. He's bright and talented. Brandon can really go places… and I'm nearly forty."

His dad rolled his eyes. "Try approaching seventy and then we'll talk. Look, son, you can do whatever you want, but please be careful. That whole business with Angus nearly did you in, and it aged your mother and me ten years in a few weeks. None of us want to go through anything like that again." He swatted Thomas's leg. "With that said, neither of us wants you to be unhappy. So follow your heart, just be careful." He huffed and chuckled. "Damn, I sound like one of those Hallmark movies your mother is always watching."

Thomas had to laugh. "I know what I want, Dad. I just haven't had any luck finding it."

"No. You may know what you want—you always seemed to have that gift—but you never looked for it, so the person you needed never found you. Love doesn't just plop in your lap like some saloon hooker in an old Western. You have to look for it, then recognize it when it comes along, put in an effort, and nurture it so it can grow. Not just hope it's going to be perfect from the start."

"Great analogy, Dad," Thomas deadpanned, then smiled. "You should write greeting cards or something."

"Stop it." Thankfully his dad had a good sense of humor. "But I'm right. You worked and did little else for years, and when Angus pursued you, he was convenient and you let yourself get involved with someone you shouldn't have."

"I know, Dad. I stayed away from everyone after that and worked harder." And that had turned out so damn well. Thomas very nearly had ulcers and was on medication for hypertension because he'd worked so hard for years and oversaw so much of the work at his company.

"Yes. Now you're here and you're stepping away from the business a little and trying to build a life. So do it. If you want my advice, be careful, but go out there and get yourself a life. Your mother and I are doing fine right now. We don't have money worries, and we're happy. Our health is only going to last so long…." His father hesitated.

"What is it?"

Dad sighed. "I want to take your mom to Australia. She's always wanted to go and it's a long trip, but I'd really like to take her before we get much older and can't."

Thomas grinned. "Then take her. Book the flights, the tour you want to take—heck, fly to Hawaii, stay a week, and then fly on from there. Do you and Mom want to take a cruise around the continent?" He met his dad's gaze as tears ran down his dad's cheeks. "Go ahead and decide what the two of you want and let me know." His mom and dad had never asked for anything from him before. He was happy to do this for them. "Plan it and we'll go over everything and get it booked."

"That's the thing. If we go, then you'll take care of the dogs?"

This was about the dogs? His dad was worried about the danged dogs?

Thomas shook his head. "I can't. Brandon works out of my house and he is highly allergic to them. He had major breathing issues just being in your house for ten minutes. And since my home is also his work environment… I can't do that. But we'll figure something out." Heck, he'd ship the little nippers to New York and Marjorie could take care of them. She loved dogs. "Don't let that stop you."

His dad smiled, his expression unreadable, and Thomas wondered what his father was so dang pleased about, other than the obvious. "Son…." He breathed. "You can't take the dogs in six or eight months because your assistant, the one you're going out with tonight, is allergic."

"Well, yeah." Granted, he wasn't sure if Brandon would still be working for him then, but he wouldn't commit to taking the dogs if Brandon might be there.

"When was the last time you let anyone tell you what to do?" His father cocked his eyebrows upward.

"You didn't let Collin dictate what happened in your apartment. Remember that week your mother and I spent with you? Collin pitched such a fit when he found out we weren't staying in a hotel, but you held your ground for us and told him to jump in the lake if he didn't like it. I know it's not the same thing, but you're already making allowances in your life for Brandon." His dad nodded slowly. "This guy must be pretty special."

"He is, Dad. I think he is." Thomas blinked and stood to wander slowly through the small space. "And I'm trying to make the most of it while it's here to be made the most of." God, that was a convoluted thought. "You understand what I'm saying?"

"I do." His dad finished his soda and tossed the can in the trash.

Thomas sat back down and finished his drink, then said goodbye to his dad and went into the house to kiss his mom on the cheek before he headed home.

He watched a baseball game that afternoon, and the Rockies won. Then he showered and changed into something nice, but not too dressy, to take Brandon to dinner. He kept expecting his phone to ring, but it stayed quiet, and without looking a gift horse in the mouth, he drove to Brandon's grandmother's and walked up to the door.

A deep male voice drifted out. "I don't know how you can live this way and why you insist on enabling him! This needs to stop, and he needs to get some help."

Thomas knocked.

"This is my house and you can leave if you can't be civil." Definitely Thelma.

Thomas knocked again and the voices went quiet. The door was opened a few seconds later by a woman probably ten years older than him.

"May I help you?" she asked nervously.

"Thomas, please come in," Thelma said, and he nodded and went inside. Thelma was pale, and Brandon was green around the edges and looked about ready to be sick.

"You know how I feel about all this, Mother," a man with Brandon's jawline and the same intensity in his eyes said.

"You know," Thelma said as she stood from the sofa, "I don't care how you feel about anything." She shook her head. "How did I raise the world's biggest bigoted asshole?" Apparently this fight was important enough to have in front of strangers. Thelma looked about ready to spit nails, so Thomas stayed near the door, out of the line of fire. "Thomas, my son and his wife were just leaving."

"This discussion isn't over," Brandon's father said.

"Yes, it is, Dad," Brandon countered. "I'm an adult with my own life, and there's nothing you can do about it." He crossed his arms over his chest. "I don't care what people say at your lodge meetings or at whatever church group you lead." An almost maniacal look spread across his face. "You have no power here. Begone… before someone drops a house on you."

Thomas grinned. "Great reference," he said, catching Brandon's gaze and earning a faint upward turn of his mouth.

"And you are?" Brandon's father asked. "One of Brandon's *friends*? Aren't you a little old for—"

"Phillip," Brandon's stepmother cautioned.

"How do I know what Brandon is doing now? Maybe this is how he paid his way through college." Phillip's eyes grew dark and hateful, a chill bracing the air.

Brandon paled and turned even more green.

"Thomas Stepford," he said, standing tall but not offering his hand. This wasn't someone he wanted to get to know better. "And you've been asked to leave." He opened the door and held it. "I suggest you do."

"I'm not done here."

Thomas glared at Brandon's father. This was going to get ugly. "Look, you can either leave like you were asked, or I can take out the trash, and that will involve shoving your dumb ass into one of the garbage cans and rolling it to the curb." He wasn't going to take this kind of shit from some idiot with a Napoleon complex. Brandon had said his father didn't support him, but to be this hostile to his own son and to his mother was way out of line. "Get going," Thomas added forcefully.

He waited, and then Brandon's father passed, his face red. Thomas jumped forward a little. Brandon's father started and yipped like a purse-dog. It was beautiful. He closed the door after Brandon's stepmother, and Thelma turned to Thomas.

"I'm sorry about all that, but thank you." She took his hand. "My son has turned into a real piece of work." She sighed. "What did I do wrong?"

"Grandma." Brandon hugged her and got her to her chair. "You need to rest. Dad is an ass most of the time. All he wants is to get his own way. Nothing

else seems to matter." Brandon stepped back. "Do you want me to make you some tea or something?"

"No. You two go on. Phillip isn't going to be back tonight, and don't let him ruin your plans." She was clearly trying to put what had happened behind her for Brandon's sake, but Brandon hadn't moved. Thelma patted his hand. "It's okay, honey. You know your father is pretty much a dick of epic proportions." She clicked her teeth. "I swear I didn't drop him on his head, though if I had, he might have turned out better."

"Grandma," Brandon said with a gasp, putting his hand over his mouth. "He's—"

She took Brandon's hand. "He's my son, but I didn't raise him to be a bigot. That's all on him. Now go have a good time. Your father doesn't get to have a say in my life, and you shouldn't let him have a say in yours." She smiled, and Brandon's color slowly returned to normal. "Go on."

"Okay," Brandon agreed. "But you call if he comes back or if you need anything."

She rolled her eyes. "I'm perfectly fine and can handle your father on my own. Like you said, he has no power here."

Brandon hugged her, and Thomas waited a few minutes while Brandon finished getting ready, and then they left the house.

"Sorry about all that. My dad is a control freak. Grandma said she spoiled him as a kid, so he's used to getting what he wants…. He's mean when he doesn't."

"What about your stepmother?" Thomas asked, opening the passenger door and holding it for Brandon. He closed it after Brandon was inside and went around to get in the black BMW.

"I don't know how she can stand it." Brandon shrugged as Thomas started the engine, the air-conditioning kicking in, cooling the interior. "I can't believe he thought you were paying me."

"Well, I am," Thomas quipped. "Not the way he thought of, the dirty-minded geezer."

"Yeah… but… he insinuated that I paid for college by being a whore." Brandon shook in his seat. "I know it's just one of my father's ways of trying to win every argument or fight he perceives. He has a paper-thin skin, and when attacked in any way, he comes out all guns blazing. It's so embarrassing. Most people give up and give him what he wants just to keep him quiet."

"Then it works," Thomas said. "He gets exactly what he wants and goes on his merry way." He grinned devilishly. "Isn't going to work with me. I have resources he could only dream of." Thomas was already formulating ways he could make Phillip's life miserable, starting with the various oversight boards. He was no Boy Scout and knew how to play hardball when the situation called for it. "Now, how about we talk about something else?" Thomas reached over and patted Brandon's leg. "I made a reservation at Ryland's Steak House. They apparently have the best food in the area."

Brandon whistled. "That's…. You don't mess around, do you? I've heard of it, of course, but I've never been there." Brandon settled back in his seat, smiling softly. "What was it like growing up here and then moving to New York?"

"Culture shock for a few months." Thomas smiled as he remembered the adjustment time. "It's loud and fast and no one waits for anyone else. It took me weeks to just be able to sleep. There's always this low-grade noise in the background. But I really did love it. I was younger then, about your age, and it was exciting and new. I thought I was ready to take on the world." Thomas shook his head.

"I take it that wasn't the case?" Brandon asked.

"God, no. But I had a real leg up. For a few years, I'd been working with Kornan Marsh. He and I had partnered on a couple of developments here in Colorado. That's how I got my start in larger projects. Kornan and I developed a project here in town and a couple up in Telluride. They were hugely successful, and he proposed that we work together in New York. Kornan was getting older and looking to retire in a few years." Thomas pulled into the lot and right up to the valet station. He gave the valet the keys, and they went inside the rich, dark-toned restaurant and gave the hostess his name. They were shown to their table and settled with menus.

"So, what happened with Kornan? You can't leave me in the middle of a story." Brandon was smiling, and it was good to see that some of the effects of the confrontation with his father seemed to have died away,

"When I first moved to New York, he took more of the lead on the projects we did together, but over time, I took that role. Kornan did more than just the projects we worked on, and eventually, after I took over the leadership role, he could have more development things in the works at once. Everything worked out for both of us. When he decided to get ready to retire, he wound down the development side of his business and I took over a lot of what he left behind."

"Didn't he have family?" Brandon asked.

Thomas scoffed and shook his head. "He had a son who was as useful as tits on a boar. All he wanted to do was spend what his dad made. Kornan's daughter is a doctor in New York, very successful, but she has her own career, so Kornan consolidated his estate. When he died, he left most of his things to his son and daughter, but he willed me the paintings at the house. They hung in his office. Both of them were so him...." Thomas swallowed around the lump in his throat. "He was good to me, and I see him when I look at those works." Thomas sniffed, picking up his menu. He was covering up, but dammit.... "The filet is supposed to be amazing." Thomas lowered his menu to find Brandon staring at him.

"You always seem so together and in-charge." Brandon smiled slightly.

Thomas didn't know what to say. He was used to hiding his emotions. In negotiations, they could give someone else the edge they needed, and he never did that. "None of us are in charge of everything all the time." He leaned forward. "Kornan was like a second father and... he was gay."

Brandon's mouth hung open for a second. "Did his children know?"

Thomas shook his head. "He was of a different generation and time. He told me he'd been married to his wife for almost forty years and never cheated or strayed. After she died, he was able to explore who he was. I think he came to grips with himself before he died, but I don't know if he was ever with another man. At least not in the time I knew him. If he was, he never told me, and I like to think he would have."

"The two of you were never together?" Brandon asked gently.

"No. He was too much of a father figure for me." Thomas picked up his menu again. "I always hoped Kornan would find someone, but...." Thomas shrugged.

"Do you think he was happy?"

Thomas thought a moment. "Yes. He was. Especially the last six months." He tried to think back, and realized that Kornan had been different the last months of his life. He smiled more and had a light in his eyes that wasn't there before. "Maybe he had found something to fill his life." He didn't want to jump to the conclusion that Kornan had found someone, but it was nice to think he had. Thomas reached across the table and took Brandon's hand, smiling at him. "You made me remember something happy."

"Good evening, gentlemen. I'm Serge. Can I get you something from the bar?"

"Yes. A bottle of sparkling wine. And please bring some water, if you would. Thank you." Thomas waited for Serge to leave and then turned to Brandon. "That's enough about me. I want to know about you. What is it you want? Really want. I know it isn't to be my assistant."

"You know I went to business school and got an MBA, but as an undergrad, I also worked in film. I found out pretty quickly that my behind-the-camera work wasn't good enough. I really don't have the eye for it. But I'd love to work in film promotion and financing." Brandon smiled. "Three years ago, we had to do a senior project. A group of us decided to make a film."

"But you said you weren't very good."

Brandon nodded and chuckled under his breath. "I was pretty awful. My job was marketing and promotion. We made the film, and I put together a marketing plan, even got a few sponsors and created a website for it. Eventually we uploaded the completed film to YouTube and ended up getting hundreds of thousands of hits. It wasn't full-length or anything, but a studio ended up picking up the rights. The other guys rewrote the script for a full-length feature, and shooting starts in a few months."

"That's impressive. They got their shot because of what you did." Thomas shook his head in awe.

"No. They got their shot because they're talented as hell. I helped them get noticed. I'd hoped that with all the business credentials, I could use that to help get Hollywood interested in me. So far it hasn't happened."

Serge brought their wine and refilled their water.

"I can't believe how thirsty I am all the time here." Thomas drank most of his water, and Serge refilled his glass once again.

"I guess I'm used to it. Most people don't realize that we're mostly desert here and it's really dry." Brandon drank as well. "Regular hydration is just part of the day." He perused his menu, and Thomas did the same. "I think I'll take your advice and have the filet."

"What sides interest you?"

"Sweet potato, maybe the beans. What do you like?" Brandon looked at him through those long lashes, and Thomas's stomach flipped a little.

"All of the above. You pick what you like. They're big enough to share, I'm sure." Thomas set aside his menu, and they placed their order when Serge returned. As soon as he was gone, Thomas leaned forward a little. "Tell me more about this film?"

"I guess my dream was to work in Hollywood. I have inquiries in with all the major players, and the guys have told me they'd put in a word for me whenever they can. I keep waiting and hoping, but I suspect that since I haven't heard anything in months, my inquiries have gone dead and I need to look in another direction." Brandon shrugged, but Thomas could tell some light had gone out of his eyes.

"Don't give up on anything," Thomas said as their salads arrived. "Send more—pepper them with inquiries if you have to. Sometimes it just takes getting noticed." He smiled. He knew success would take Brandon away, but he wanted him to be happy. That was what was important when caring for someone.

They ate their salads, and then the main courses arrived. There was plenty of food, and Thomas ate until he was totally stuffed. The steak was seasoned to perfection and melted in his mouth, but the highlight of the meal were the soft hums of gustatory delight that sent heat through Thomas. And the way Brandon closed his eyes when he took a bite had a lot more than food running through Thomas's mind.

"Jeez, that must be really good." He smiled at Brandon.

"It is. I spent so much of the last few years eating whatever I could to get by on a student's budget. As you saw today, Dad wasn't going to help, and I couldn't ask Grandma. She needs what she gets for herself. So I got by as best I could."

"Brandon," Thomas said as he put down his knife and fork and took Brandon's hand, massaging his fingers lightly. "You have the biggest heart. Most people would take whatever they could get to make their life easier."

Brandon shook his head. "I couldn't do that, not to her. I did what I had to in order to get through school, including spending long days studying, working part-time jobs, and earning teaching-aid stipends. All of it. By the time I got through school, I'd been hoping to get a really good job and...."

"You ended up as my assistant." Thomas had known this was never Brandon's dream job, but he hadn't understood how much he'd settled.

"Not that working for you isn't a good job." Brandon blushed adorably. Thomas loved that look. It meant Brandon couldn't lie, and it showed who he truly was.

"I know. You have dreams of your own." Thomas released his fingers and pulled out his phone, looking for a specific picture, and then handed it to Brandon. "That was my dream."

"Your name on a building?" Brandon said as he moved the phone closer to his face.

"Yeah. We all want something that will last past us and endure. This was the first major project that I did after Kornan died, and I put my name on it because I did it on my own. It was my conception, and I brought it to fruition. I had thought to take one of the penthouse apartments at the top, but I stayed where I was and put them all up for sale. The next project I named for Kornan. He'd have hated it, but it made me happy to remember him." Thomas put the phone away.

"What's your dream now?" Brandon asked.

Thomas opened his mouth, but no words came out. He found he didn't really have one. He'd been running his business for so long and immersed himself so much that he'd lost sight of anything else. "I don't know." Thomas picked up his fork again. "I think part of why I'm here is to try to find a new one." He smiled. "But I think I'm going to help my mom and dad with one of theirs. They've talked about traveling for years and want to go to Australia, so they're going to plan it, and in the winter, Australian summer, they can go."

"Sounds awesome. Do you need help?" Brandon asked, like a good assistant.

"No. Mom and Dad are deciding what they want to do, and then we'll get a travel agent to help plan the whole thing for them."

"I'd love to go there sometime. Snorkeling on the Great Barrier Reef, koalas, Sydney Harbour, kangaroos, all of it." Brandon's eyes lit up with excitement. "I never really got much of a chance to travel. Dad and Mom used to take a vacation every winter. It was a 'just the two of them' vacation, and I stayed with Grandma."

"They never took you?" Thomas was shocked. His parents had always taken him everywhere with them, and each summer they'd gone somewhere special.

"Not on those trips. We went on driving vacations nearby in the summer, but they went to the Caribbean or to Mexico during the winter, and those were for them." Brandon bit his lower lip. "I used to like it because I got to spend time with Grandma, but it was hard being left behind, knowing I wasn't welcome." He sighed.

"Sounds a little like something your dad would do." Thomas tried to make light of it. "You know the good part about growing up? We can make up for the things we didn't get when we were kids." Thomas raised his eyebrows, and Brandon smiled, dispelling the pall created by the mention of his father.

"I'll get to travel, though. Once I get a more permanent job, I hope I can afford some interesting trips in a few years."

"Have you thought about dessert?" Serge asked.

Brandon shook his head. "I'm way too full for anything like that."

"Me too," Thomas said.

Serge returned with the check, and Thomas paid the bill. Then they left the restaurant, stepping outside.

"Do you want to take a walk?"

"Sure. Are we going to see a movie or something?"

"We can. But when I was out this week, I found this restaurant, and then I continued down the street." Thomas took Brandon's hand, heading west. "I forgot about this view and what it looked like." They walked beyond the buildings to a rise, and the city fell away behind them and the landscape opened up. Pikes Peak rose in the distance, the sun setting behind it, coloring the sky in a full palate of color.

"I used to come out here all the time when I was a kid." Brandon squeezed his hand. "When I was in school, we used to sing 'America the Beautiful' and I knew where those words came from. It had to be right here." Brandon leaned against him, and Thomas put his arm around Brandon's shoulders, standing still for a few seconds and then turning toward him. Their gazes met, pulling them closer until they kissed, sending a spark of desire racing through him.

"I know. This really is purple mountain majesty." Thomas kissed Brandon again because it felt too perfect not to. His head swam a little, and he let it float. Being bone-deep contented and happy was such a new experience for him. For years happiness came at the end of an adrenaline ride of contacts, construction, problem-solving, and late nights powered by coffee and takeout. This was so different. Thomas deepened the kiss, inhaling Brandon's amazingly clean scent, loving the soft soundtrack of happiness that Brandon provided.

A car honked on the street behind them, startling them both. Brandon moved away, and Thomas groaned softly. "Maybe we should move on." He took Brandon's hand, and they walked toward the car.

THE MOVIE was fine, though Thomas didn't remember much about it. He and Brandon sat in the back and spent more time kissing like teenagers than watching what was actually happening on-screen. When the lights came up, they both grinned and left the theater as quickly as possible.

"Man, I don't think I've ever watched a movie like that."

Thomas smiled. "Movie? I don't remember a movie."

Brandon took Thomas's hand as they walked. Thomas turned to look at their entwined fingers. "I should probably take you home." He didn't want to press, and maybe taking things in a more measured way was best.

"Thomas." Brandon stopped. "Yes, take me to your home." The heat in his eyes left no doubt about what Brandon wanted.

They reached the car, and Thomas drove them back to his house. The laughter slowly died away, replaced by tension and anticipation the closer they got to the house. Sure, they'd spent a few hours making out in the theater, but that had its limits. But now at his house, with a bed just upstairs, the possibilities were endless, and by the time they got inside, the air between them crackled with unspoken desire.

Thomas closed the door, wishing he had the words to be able to ask just what Brandon had in mind. He turned, catching Brandon's heated gaze. His body thrummed with desire, but he didn't dare move closer, or the last threads of control would snap. He had to know what Brandon wanted. Thomas had been here before, and part of him was scared as hell. Before, this moment had been just as heady, which was the problem. He needed to think with his big head and not his little one.

"Thomas," Brandon said quietly. "I can see the confusion in your eyes. You don't need to worry so much." He moved even closer, and Thomas tugged at the collar of his shirt as the temperature in the room jumped. "Everything is going to be great." Brandon kissed him gently, and Thomas dropped his hands to his sides, not daring to touch Brandon. Instead, he let him take the lead, and what a lead Brandon took.

He wrapped his arms around Thomas's neck, drawing them together. Thomas raised his arms slowly and wrapped them around Brandon's waist. Brandon kissed him harder, ramping up the intensity, tugging on Thomas's lips until the threads broke and he crushed Brandon to him, feasting on his lips as he slowly moved them through the house.

Suddenly it was a tempest, the two of them vying for control, feet fumbling as they made their way toward the stairs. Waves of desire and winds of passion blew them from wall to wall and step to step. They nearly tumbled to the floor on multiple occasions, but neither of them seemed to care and only held on tighter, until they made it to Thomas's bedroom door, banging it on the stops in a bid to get inside.

Thomas's shirt parted, and he let go of Brandon to yank it off, then tugged Brandon's polo up and off as well. They fluttered to the floor somewhere as Thomas closed the distance between them once again, bare chest to bare chest. Thomas rubbed against Brandon like a cat, needing to feel his skin against his. Shoes twirled through the air as they kicked them off, and Thomas propelled them the last few feet to the bed. It groaned under their combined weight falling on it, and then there was only the two of them.

Brandon paused, pulling away slightly, his eyes meeting Thomas's. Thomas held still, not wanting to move for fear this would pop like a soap bubble. "God, you take my breath away." Brandon blinked, then tilted his head forward to run his tongue over Thomas's nipple. He quivered and shook as Brandon sucked and worked the bud until Thomas could barely see straight. "I see someone is sensitive."

"Uh-huh…." Thomas gasped as Brandon slowly worked his fingers over his belly and down to his belt. Instead of going where Thomas expected, they veered off to the sides, grazing over his abs, then traveling upward. Damn, that was…. Thomas quivered again, closing his eyes to take in the ripples of unexpected desire. "Don't stop." He was like a desert getting the first gentle rain in months, soaking in each drop as it fell. Too much and it would run off, but Brandon knew just what to give. Thomas soaked it in, Brandon refilling what had been cruelly taken away all those years ago. Thomas hadn't realized how parched his soul was until Brandon slowly began refilling it.

Thomas closed his arms around Brandon once more, their lips coming together as Thomas slid his hands down Brandon's rippling back and over his hips and sides until he reached his belt. He opened it between them, fumbling to loosen the catch. Then he parted the fabric and slid his hands under the material and over Brandon's smooth butt, cupping his cheeks as he pressed him closer.

Brandon's hips undulated, and Thomas pressed upward, his cock throbbing in its confinement. Their kissing grew sloppy and rushed. Brandon pulled away, arching his back as Thomas massaged his butt. God, this was heady—raw and uncontrollable. Not that Thomas wanted to try to contain what was happening between them. Each second added a new sensation that grew on top of the last.

He groaned as Brandon ground against him, hips rolling. Thomas did his best to get some more of Brandon's clothes off, but he wasn't having much luck. Brandon sighed and rolled away, shucking his pants in a flurry of kicking legs and feet. Thomas didn't move as fast, and once Brandon was naked, he slipped Thomas's pants off before bounding onto him, the mattress bouncing.

"You have so much energy."

"I hope so." Brandon grinned and kissed Thomas deeply, pressing him into the mattress as a rush of desire raced through Thomas. Holding Brandon was like grabbing a live wire. He was so filled with energy, Thomas wasn't sure he could compete with it. Not that he needed to, considering Brandon seemed to have enough for the both of them. So Thomas held him tightly, returning his energetic kisses, and got lost in the passion that Brandon exuded in every direction.

"Damn," Thomas moaned as Brandon slid down him, lips and hands making trails across his skin, leaving behind a line of fading heat that had Thomas shaking with barely controlled desire. Thomas gripped the bedding, then gave up and let himself ride the waves of passion.

"What do you like, Thomas?" Brandon wound his fingers around his cock, gripping him tightly, stroking slowly.

"Brandon," he whimpered, and instantly wondered where that sound had come from.

"Thomas." Brandon leaned closer, their gazes locking. "What makes your head spin and your heart race in your ears?"

Thomas swallowed hard, unable to breathe. "I want you," he managed to eke out as his throat dried.

Brandon leaned over until his lips were right next to Thomas's. "You want to bury this thick cock inside me? Is that what you want?" he whispered, and Thomas groaned deep in his throat. "I'm right, aren't I?"

"Yeah." Thomas hugged Brandon tight and rolled them on the bed. He loved the way Brandon felt under him, shaking as Thomas let his hands wander over Brandon's acres of smooth, gorgeous skin covering long, lean muscle. "Sweetheart, you're stunning beyond belief." He could barely believe Brandon was here with him, looking at him like he hung the moon. Being the center of Brandon's attention was mind-blowing. Thomas groaned when Brandon gasped, his pert nipple sliding between Thomas's fingers. Oh yes, he was worth waiting for. Thomas shifted down to kiss Brandon, smoothing his hands along his sides and hips to cup his ass in his hands.

"Fuck, Thomas, I want…."

"Oh yeah." Thomas slowly rocked back and forth. Brandon wrapped his long legs around Thomas's waist, and they moved as one. He wondered if he was ever going to get enough of Brandon, then realized he wanted all of him, all at the same time. Thomas couldn't get enough of him. Every taste made him want more. Every touch, and all he wanted was another. "Me too." He didn't want to let go of Brandon, even long enough to get the supplies so he could sink into this hot, gorgeous man with sunshine in his eyes.

Thomas tried to remember if he *had* supplies. It wasn't like he'd expected this, though he probably should have. He stopped, looking toward the bedside table.

Brandon rolled his eyes and reached to pull the drawer open. "Your assistant was efficient and took care of things for just such an occasion."

"Oh, he did, huh?" Thomas reached inside and found the things he needed. "I think I'll have to remember to thank him. Maybe I can send a thank-you card. I wonder if Hallmark makes 'thank you for buying condoms' cards?"

Brandon smacked his shoulder. "Ass." He laughed, and Thomas went right along with him. It was amazing to kid and joke while making love. That—and so much more—had been missing from his life.

"Smarty-pants…." Thomas had to come up with something.

"More like 'smarty-no-pants' at the moment." Brandon tugged him down into a kiss, and whatever else he was thinking flew from Thomas's mind. He dropped the lube and condom on the mattress, feasting on Brandon's sweetness.

"I think I like Mr. Smarty-No-Pants," he said, then kissed Brandon once again.

"Thomas," Brandon breathed after a few minutes. "I want you. Grab that condom and fuck me. I know you're being gentle and caring, but I want you, and I want you to roll on that latex and fuck me into next week."

Thomas fumbled on the bedding for the condom, found the damned square packet, ripped it open, and rolled it on himself with shaking hands. Once he was sheathed, he found the lube and made sure they were both ready before getting into position, his gaze locked on Brandon, and sliding forward.

Brandon was gorgeous and the heat surrounding Thomas was incredible, but that was nothing compared to the intense passion burning in Brandon's eyes. He never looked away, watching Thomas as he sank deeper into him. Brandon wound his arms around Thomas's neck, holding him close as their bodies connected in the most primal, soul-touching experience of Thomas's life. His heart warmed, and he realized something so basic and eye-opening after forty years: a connection and emotions mattered. He'd heard that all his life, but he realized he'd never experienced it. He thought he had before, but that was nothing like this. *Sex* had never been like this before. Thomas listened to Brandon's breath, his own synchronizing with it just as his body took its cues from him. For a fleeting few seconds, he wondered what he was going to do without this. Thomas pushed that away as the intensity grew between them. Each touch and movement sent him higher and pushed at the last of his control. He wanted this to go on as long as possible, but Brandon was too hot, and the way his skin glistened in the soft light, combined with his intensely sexy scent, pushed Thomas closer to release by the second.

Thomas waited, watching Brandon's eyes until they shone and his breath hitched. Brandon stilled and tightened around him, his release wracking him, propelling Thomas over the edge. He held still, not wanting to move, wishing everything could stay as blissful and perfect as this one single moment.

Chapter 8

BRANDON FLOATED on cloud nine the next week. Thomas worked but kept what he did to normal hours, and Brandon oversaw the people who came in to clean and took care of whatever Thomas needed during work hours. During the day, they worked professionally, keeping Thomas on schedule and making sure he was ready for his conference calls and other meetings. In the evenings, they went out sometimes or just stayed in and had some quiet time for the two of them. Brandon almost always went home to check on his grandmother rather than staying the night. He didn't want her to think she'd been abandoned.

He found one of the neighbor kids to mow the lawn. Harv reminded Brandon of himself at that age, and it turned out he did really good work. The front lawn got mowed when it needed it, and the beds near the house were weeded and looked fresh. There was no grass in the back, just desert landscaping and plenty of outdoor living space, which Harv had weeded and freshened up.

An entire week without drama....

"Morning, Marjorie," Brandon said happily on Monday morning as he got ready to head out to do Thomas's shopping. "Thomas is in a meeting right now." He was about to pull the door closed, but paused.

"I figured as much. He isn't answering his calls, and I need to speak with him." Her voice shook, which told Brandon this call was anything but normal. "Blaze has been trying to get in touch with him too, but his phone goes right to voicemail."

"He's on one of the calls on his calendar."

"Look, please pop your head in and get his attention. He'll understand that it's something important and wrap up the call to find out what you need. If you have to, use my name. He'll understand." She really seemed to be at the end of her rope.

Brandon went back inside. "Hold on." He set his phone on the table outside the room and poked his head in the office.

Thomas had his phone on speaker, listening intently. When he looked up, Brandon caught his gaze, and he muted the call. "Yes?" He didn't sound too happy.

"Marjorie said to interrupt. Call her, and she said Blaze has been trying to call you too. It sounds really important." Brandon closed the door and picked up his phone. "I got his attention. What else do you need me to do?"

She sighed heavily, which was also unlike her. "Be prepared for yelling." She ended the call, and

Brandon set his phone aside, putting off his shopping trip to be close by in case Thomas needed him. Instead, he sat at the kitchen counter, making a list of what he wanted to get done.

A growl broke the silence, and Brandon jumped. He'd thought Marjorie had been kidding about the yelling, but apparently not. He slid off the stool, heading to the office.

"You have got to be kidding me! We have all the details documented and ironed out. That little bastard is trying this crap now? I'll wring his slimy little neck."

Brandon had thought to see if he could help, but he returned to the kitchen to stay out of the line of fire. He thought his family was bad…. The anger that rolled out of that office and through the rest of the house was as black as storm clouds.

"I have the letters of intent right here, and if he thinks he's going to back out, I'll sue him for everything he has and drag his name through more mud than a Louisiana flash flood!"

Quiet followed and hung in the air for a few minutes. Brandon kept expecting another outburst, but the house stayed silent, which rattled his nerves a little.

"Blaze, you need to play hardball with this guy. I'll give the lawyers a call, and have Harry and Dean in there. When you have this meeting, I want them flanking you." Thomas strode into the kitchen and yanked open the refrigerator door so hard, the jars rattled and threatened to fall out. "Where's the water!" he barked.

Brandon weaved around him, pushed aside the orange juice, and handed a bottle to Thomas, who stalked back toward his door.

"If you really think you need me, then I'll be there. I want this meeting set up for no later than Wednesday morning, but have Marjorie do it and tell her that we're already preparing a bill for all expenses and delay costs per the letter of intent. Make sure they know that the bill is starting at about twenty thousand and going up by that amount each day. She'll know how to throw that in to make them panic. Then she can tell them that we can meet on Wednesday morning." Thomas closed his office door, and Brandon sure as hell didn't want to be on the receiving end of whatever Thomas had in mind. It sounded pretty ugly.

Brandon had things he needed to get done for Thomas, and hanging around here wasn't going to get them accomplished. Thomas seemed ensconced in his office, so he left a note on the counter and hurried outside. He headed right to the grocery store and got a cart. He'd reached the produce section to check out the strawberries that Thomas loved when his phone rang.

"Hey, Thomas. I'm at the store."

"I need you back at the house right away. So drop what you're doing and come right back," Thomas said, then hung up.

Brandon hurried back to the car. He'd taken a chance that he'd be able to get something done, and it looked like all his plans had been thrown up in the air.

"Brandon." Thomas met him at the door with the phone still in his hand. "I need you to call Marjorie and have her get us to New York. She'll know how to make the arrangements. Then go on up and pack me a bag with my best power suits, and get bags packed for yourself. We'll need to leave as soon as possible, so hurry."

"Do you want hotel rooms?"

"Tell Marjorie that we'll stay in one of our apartments that's vacant. The best available." Thomas walked into his office, and Brandon called Marjorie as he headed for Thomas's bedroom.

"Is he coming?" Marjorie asked as soon as she answered the phone.

"Yes. We need a flight, and he said to get us into one of the vacant apartments. The best one available. He didn't want to stay in a hotel."

"I'll check and see what there is. The plane is in Denver already, so I just need to make a call. Get him packed, and I'll get right back to you." Then she was gone.

Brandon went to Thomas's closet and laid out the suits he thought Thomas would look the most intimidating in, along with the rest of the clothes he'd need. He wanted Thomas to review them before he did the actual packing. By the time he was done, Marjorie called back.

"The plane is set and will be ready in three hours. I don't have any apartments at the moment, other than some smaller ones that aren't going to do. I have a suite booked at the Plaza for the two of you."

Brandon made notes as Marjorie sent him texts. "I don't understand why he wants me with him when he'll have you." Not that he was complaining.

"At times like this, it's complete chaos. I'll be running everything here. Your job is to make sure everything runs as smoothly with him as possible. Just get him ready, put it on the company card, and get him here."

"Yes, boss." He smiled and hung up, hurrying back to the kitchen as Thomas emerged from his office. "I have your clothes on your bed. Please make sure it's what you want, and I'll pack it." He went into Thomas's office, found his chargers, and plugged everything in so they would be ready.

"The clothes look great. I added a few things."

"Then I'll pack them, and then I need to run and pack myself. Marjorie said the plane will leave in three hours. So we need to be ready in an hour." He grabbed his phone and left, calling his grandma, telling her what was happening. She met him at the door and helped him pack.

"How long will you be gone?" his grandma asked, handing him a couple of brand-new shirts in the packages. "I got these for your birthday next month, but they might be good for you." She placed them on the bed, and Brandon went through his suits. He had a few, but nothing like the immaculately tailored ones Thomas had. "I like this one."

Brandon agreed and packed the dove gray, as well as the deep blue and charcoal ones. He laid out ties and the other clothes he thought he'd need, including casual things in case he ended up running errands for Thomas. Then he packed a garment bag and suitcase and brought them to the living room. "I'll call you as soon as I get there, and if you need anything, call me or Thomas's parents. They'll know where we are and will be able to provide any help you need."

She waved away the notion. "I'll be fine. I spent enough time alone to be able to handle things for a few days." She hugged him. "Be safe and do a good job."

When she released him, Brandon checked his watch and raced back to Thomas's as fast as he dared. He transferred his bags to Thomas's car, went inside, and carried out Thomas's before packing the computer bag Marjorie had sent with the laptop, putting in all the devices he'd need.

"Thomas, do you need anything else?" he asked when he found him in the office.

"No." Thomas put some papers in his bag. "This is the last of it. Lock up the back, and we'll get going." They headed in different directions, and once the house was locked and checked, they met at the front door and walked out to the car.

"Are we going to make it on time?" Brandon asked as he checked the time—a little over two hours left.

"No problem. You drive so I can make calls." Thomas got into the passenger seat, and Brandon slipped behind the wheel of the sweet BMW and started the engine. "The pilot isn't going to take off until we're on board, considering you and I are the only passengers." Thomas grinned, and what Marjorie had said about the single suite at the Plaza clicked. They were going to be the only occupants of the single hotel suite as well. That was definitely going to be interesting.

"Are we going in your plane?" Brandon knew Thomas was wealthy, but he hadn't given much thought to just how much money he had.

"It's the business's plane, but I have priority, and since I arrived, it's been in Denver in case I needed to get back."

Thomas sent text messages while Brandon drove. As they got closer, Thomas directed them to the private section of the airport, and once they were cleared through security, they headed out to the private jet.

"Man…." Brandon hummed as he followed Thomas on board. Their luggage was stowed for them, and they settled in plush, luxurious seats to get ready for takeoff.

"We're ready," Thomas said into a phone.

The attendant closed the door, and the plane taxied out, smoothly leaped into the sky, and turned toward the east and New York.

ONCE IN the air, Thomas spent a lot of time on the phone. Brandon wandered through the cabin a little, checking out the luxury before sitting back down. The flight was going to take nearly four hours. He checked that Thomas didn't need anything and then settled in for the ride.

Thomas grabbed his bag, pulling out some papers and setting them on the table in front of them.

"What's going on?" Brandon asked tentatively.

"One of the sellers for a project we've been working on has decided he wants to hold out, most likely for more money, and is being a dick. He has a reputation that isn't stellar, and I wouldn't deal with him if I didn't have to. But this idiot has messed with the wrong person. We made him sign a letter of intent, which is a binding contract, and I added a clause that stipulates that he pays the costs of any delays caused by him." Thomas leaned back in the chair. "And I have his signature on it. He wants to play with the big boys, well, he's going to find out that this one is a shark and

I have a huge set of teeth." He smiled, then returned his attention to the papers in front of him.

Brandon ended up reading on the iPad for a few hours. He and Thomas were treated like kings, with the flight attendant bringing drinks and generally taking care of both of them. There was internet, so Brandon texted Marjorie to let her know where they were, and she messaged back right away.

I have a car that will be waiting to take you into the city once you arrive. It's going to be late, so find out what Thomas wants to do for dinner. He can get a seat in the hotel restaurants easily, but if he wants to go somewhere else, you'll need to make a reservation. Use Open Table.

Thanks. I'll check, he sent in return. *Anything else?*

No. You'll get in late because of the time change. Get something to eat and get some rest. The next few days are going to be exhausting, and while the time change is only two hours, it's going to affect you. I'm looking forward to meeting you in person tomorrow. She sent a smiley face, and Brandon smiled, sending her one in return.

He spoke to Thomas once he was off the phone and contacted the hotel to let them know they would eat there that evening. They assured him it wouldn't be a problem. Then Brandon checked the time and rolled his eyes. It had been a very busy day and he hadn't eaten much. The attendant brought snacks and apologized that there wasn't something more. Still, the mixed nuts were good, and he ate enough of them to hold him over.

"I'm a little nervous," Brandon confessed, and Thomas lifted his gaze from his papers. "I don't know anything about New York, and I really don't know why you brought me along. It isn't like I can really help you here." Marjorie was the one who had New York wired and all, not him.

"You'll be here to help me. Stay close and take care of everything you can. These kinds of situations always get crazy. The office is going to be up in arms because they've all put a lot of time and effort into this project, and they'll be nervous and wired. Just stay calm and be available."

Brandon nodded slowly. He really wasn't sure what that meant, but he figured he could do that.

Thomas leaned back in his seat, closing his eyes. "I'm so done for now. I can't look at these papers any-more. They aren't going to tell me anything I don't already know." He sighed deeply.

Brandon slipped out from behind the table to the other side and slid into the chair next to Thomas. "Are you officially done working for now?" He took one of Thomas's hands. "You look drawn and tired."

"I am. I feel like I've been running full speed for a week. I used to be able to do that for days on end. But I can't anymore."

Brandon made a mental note to get Thomas to a doctor when they got home. "You aren't old." He squeezed his hand.

"No, I'm not. But I can't go at this pace forever. It was why I moved, and now I'm going back." Thomas bit his lower lip. "I don't want to go back to New York permanently, but I'm afraid I might have to."

Brandon's chest clenched, but he didn't release Thomas's hand. "You can live wherever you want to. You deserve that. This is one issue. We'll be there for a few days, and then you can go home." He gently turned Thomas's head to face him and kissed him softly at first, but then leaned into the magnetic touch, wanting more. "Let yourself look forward to that."

"I'm doing my best, but maybe I was too hasty moving out to Colorado when I did. Maybe I should have spent more time making sure everyone was ready for this."

Brandon sighed. "As long as you were in New York, they were never going to be ready for it. They rely on you quite a bit." He'd seen that more than once, especially with the number of phone calls Thomas received through the day.

"Gentlemen, we'll be landing in half an hour," the attendant said as everything in the cabin was prepped for touchdown.

"Everything is going to be great. You know that. This guy doesn't stand a chance." Brandon wished he could do more for Thomas, but he wasn't someone involved in the day-to-day running of his business and didn't know enough about it to be helpful. As someone who cared about Thomas, he wanted him to be able to take it a little easy and let go of some of this pressure. More than anything, he wanted Thomas to be happy.

Thomas smiled, and Brandon hoped he'd helped. The last thing he wanted was for Thomas to return to New York permanently.

THEY LANDED and found a limousine waiting for them. They got in, and their bags were transferred from the plane. Brandon watched out the windows as they drove toward the city. The lights of New York seemed to come on as they rode in, the light of the day fading and the city turning itself on. Brandon switched from side to side, not wanting to miss anything.

Thomas smiled at him as Brandon got excited.

"Is that the Empire State Building?"

"Yes," Thomas answered as everything disappeared from view when they passed through one of the tunnels and then burst into Manhattan. "We're probably going to go up Fifth to the hotel, so keep a lookout."

The stores glittered, the library lions sat regally, and Rockefeller Center glowed with light as they passed. They pulled up to the entrance for the Plaza and the driver opened the door. Brandon stepped out, looking upward, his mouth hanging open at the height of elegance and grace. A chill ran up his spine, and he looked downward at himself, wondering if he was dressed well enough to pass through those doors.

He grabbed his computer bag, and Thomas put an arm around his shoulders, guiding him toward the entrance. "It's all right. It's just a fancy hotel."

"That's easy for you to say," Brandon said as his nerves increased.

Thomas chuckled and leaned close. "Remember, I'm not from here either. I grew up in the same town you did. Just put on your game face and pretend you belong here. Keep your head high, look straight ahead, and don't let anyone or anything intimidate you." Thomas squeezed him lightly, and then they walked to the door and passed inside.

The interior was even more breathtaking, with marble and stately elegance everywhere. Thomas approached the desk, and Brandon did his best not to gape about like an obvious tourist, but it was difficult. "You ready?" Thomas asked, and they walked to the elevators. "Our luggage will be brought up."

"Of course." Brandon stayed close, and they entered the elevator and the bellman pressed the floor. They rode up in a miniature cubicle of luxury, everything about this place exuding grace and elegance. Brandon had a few questions, but he was afraid to speak, and when he did, it was in his church voice. "I feel like the country cousin in a Jane Austen novel."

Thomas nodded as the door opened and they stepped out into a hallway of soothing cream, their footsteps muffled by plush carpet. The bellman unlocked the door, and they stepped inside.

"The Ellington Park Suite," the bellman whispered. "Do you need me to show you anything?"

"No. It's perfect. Thank you," Thomas said, tipping him.

"Shall I place the luggage?" He looked from the bags to each of them.

"It's all right. I'll do it. Thank you." Brandon set the computer bag carefully on the sofa. Truth be told, he was afraid to touch anything in case something happened, because he figured each piece of furniture in this breathtaking room of light blues, white, gold, and soft gray cost more than he made in a month.

"Very good." The bellman nodded and left the room.

Brandon finally allowed himself to take a breath. He felt like one of those girls in a Bond movie or something, overwhelmed by James's surroundings. "Is Marjorie nuts?" he asked.

"Why do you ask that?" Thomas lifted his garment bag and carried it into the first bedroom. Brandon peeked inside at the ultimate luxury of the king-size bed, suddenly relieved the room had a second bedroom, because he was going to need it to hide and keep his hands to himself.

"She could have just booked a couple rooms at the Hilton or something." This had to cost a fortune. Brandon tamped down his nerves and carried the rest of Thomas's bags into the bedroom and started unpacking everything. "I'm going to need to find a cleaners. Your shirts wrinkled."

"Call down to the lobby. They'll come get them and have them pressed by morning." Thomas sat on the edge of the bed. "You have nothing to be concerned about."

Brandon separated the shirts and made the call. Then he finished unpacking while Thomas made some calls, leaving the room. Brandon finished his task before returning to the living room, where he found Thomas on the sofa with the television on. When Brandon approached, he patted the seat next to him.

Thomas gestured to the other room. "Marjorie got us a two-bedroom suite. It's up to you which bedroom you want to use. I won't push you if you don't feel comfortable…."

Brandon slid closer to Thomas, leaning against him. He lifted his gaze to find Thomas looking back at him. "I don't want you to think…." He swallowed hard. "I never want you to think that I care about you… for this." He motioned around the room.

"I didn't. Marjorie made the reservations, remember?" Thomas smiled.

"She said she'd take care of it. I never mentioned that we should stay at the most expensive and famous hotel in New York." Brandon started to move away, but Thomas held him still.

"I know that. Marjorie did this on her own and got this house-sized suite because she wanted us to be comfortable and have some space. This has nothing to do with you, and I know you don't care for me because of my money. I've had that happen before—I know what it feels like."

"Good. Because I care about you for you. Not the plane or the fancy hotels." Brandon moved closer once again. "And I don't want to stay in that room way over there. I like this… right now… quiet and just you."

"Then that's what we'll do." Thomas yawned and closed his eyes. "Go ahead and get yourself settled. We'll go down to the Palm Court for some dinner. They have a nice menu, and the surroundings are magnificent."

"Okay." Brandon began to get up, but Thomas tugged him back to kiss him.

"You know, I dated someone I worked with before, and, well…. With him, things never felt like this. There was always this push-and-shove about how he should act at work and when we were alone. If he got angry, he suddenly reverted to employee status and acted like I was treating him like a servant or something. You…."

"We talked about this. No lovey-dovey hanky-panky during working hours, and right now I need to see to things. I'm sure you have a few calls to make, and I have some things to finish up. And I need to change, because I'm not walking in there looking like a schlub. Then when we leave the room, I can be your date for the evening." Brandon bounded away and took care of his luggage. His shirts were worse than Thomas's.

A soft knock sounded on the door. Brandon answered it and gave the bellman all the shirts they needed to have pressed. They were whisked away with a promise they'd be ready first thing in the morning.

Brandon put on one of his new white shirts and then his dove gray suit with a deep blue tie. He also made a pass through the marble bathroom and met Thomas in the living room.

"You look very nice."

"So do you."

Thomas put on his jacket, and they headed to the elevator. This time Brandon held Thomas's hand, and as the doors slid closed, he kept his gaze on Thomas for the ride down.

They shared a smile, and once they got off, Thomas led them to the restaurant, with its palm trees and stained-glass ceiling that took his breath away. No wonder Thomas wanted to eat here. This was a once-in-a-lifetime chance for Brandon.

They had an exquisite dinner of duck and salmon, each bite a burst of flavor. Brandon was spoiled forever. The diner back home would never be the same. "I could get used to this…," Brandon quipped as he finished his duck, sitting back full and happy.

"Tomorrow will be a long day, and it will be pizza and takeout for dinner," Thomas warned, even as he tried not to smile. He set his napkin on the table and took care of the check. Then Thomas guided him out of the restaurant and through the front door.

As soon as they stepped out, the sounds of the city nearly bowled Brandon over, noise coming at him from every direction. "How could you stand it?" Brandon resisted the urge to cover his ears.

"You get used to it, and after a while, you miss it, believe it or not. Millions of people living and working in just a few square miles." Thomas pointed to an illuminated gold statue on top of a huge pedestal. "Central Park is right over there, and if you walk down Fifth, you pass some of the world's most interesting and expensive shops. Times Square is that way, as are all the theaters of Broadway. Is there anything you want to do?"

"Do?" Brandon asked, completely overwhelmed.

"Sure. Come on." Thomas took Brandon's hand, weaving their fingers together. "I thought we could go for a walk."

The sidewalks were still jammed with people bustling down the busy thoroughfare. They passed Tiffany's, and more designer clothing stores than he'd ever seen in his life, as they walked.

"This is one of the best places in the world. I loved it here for a long time."

"Why?" Brandon asked, holding Thomas tightly in case they got separated.

"The energy. I knew if I could be a success here, I could be one anywhere in the world. Everything here is heightened, and there's pressure on top of pressure, tons of money, and…." Thomas stopped, and they turned around. "There's our hotel. Just a small portion of it is the actual hotel any longer. Mostly it's apartments that people own. They start at ten million dollars. And they're sold out. Our suite would sell for twenty million or so. And that's just the suite we're staying in tonight. It's smaller than the house your grandma lives in." He shrugged. "Everyone competes for everything here. It was like a dream of sorts to match wits with some of the best in the business and come out on top."

Brandon turned, tugging on Thomas's hand. "I thought you were on top of the world that first day when you answered the door shirtless and hired me to mow your lawn." Brandon tilted his head slightly. "You were busy and doing great things at home... and you were twenty-eight or twenty-nine. Even my mom and dad talked about how successful you were."

Thomas shrugged. "I guess I wanted more." He turned away. "And look what it got me."

"It made you a success," Brandon told him firmly, putting his hands on his hips. "And your family is proud of you. My mom and dad found out I was gay when I was in college. I couldn't hide who I was anymore, and it nearly broke my heart when they rejected me. I packed my things and left the house. Grandma gave me a permanent home because she loved me no matter what." Brandon wiped his eyes as people passed by, jostling him slightly.

"I'm sorry that happened," Thomas said.

"I'm not. It happened years ago, and I'm pretty much over it. My mom and dad aren't going to change, and I learned a lot of things because of it. I'm stronger than I thought I was, and Grandma showed just how much she loves and cares for me. I also realized that I needed to rely on myself for my happiness, not other people." Brandon caught Thomas's gaze and cupped his cheeks in his hands. "It also helped me become the person I am now and put me on the path to whoever I'm going to be. So whatever you did here and all the successes and failures only made you the man you are."

"But I spent most of those years alone, working myself most of the way to an ulcer and a chronic case of hypertension. I had one real relationship, and that...." He shuddered.

Brandon took Thomas's hands. "Maybe you can tell me what happened someday." He brushed Thomas's shoulder, and Thomas quivered. "But all of that still made you who you are."

"I suppose. Lord knows I don't want to make the same mistakes again." Thomas looked all around him.

"Do you think you're the same person you were when you first came here? As wide-eyed and overwhelmed as I am? I didn't really know you then, but let me tell you, you're not. You're stronger, harder when you need to be, smarter, and the most driven person I've ever met. You can move to Colorado Springs to try to take it easy, but the drive you have is there because of this place. New York and everything that happened made you who you are... made you the man who swept me off my feet." Brandon drew Thomas to him and kissed him.

"How did you get to be so damn smart?" Thomas asked with a smile.

Brandon snickered. "Born that way?"

They continued down the street, walking a few blocks before taking the side street and going around the block and back to the hotel. Brandon was getting tired and needed time out of the noise and bustle. What he really needed was quiet time with Thomas, and once they were back inside the room, Brandon led Thomas to the bedroom, closed the door, and pressed him back until he sat on the edge of the bed. Brandon stepped away, pulling off his tie and then slipping his jacket off his shoulders.

Thomas watched him closely; Brandon felt his gaze on him like a touch as he toed off his shoes and then loosened his collar. That felt so damn good, but not nearly as wonderful as having Thomas's undivided attention.

Brandon held out his hand, and Thomas looked at him, confused. Brandon wagged his fingers and raised an eyebrow, and Thomas reached into his pocket and handed Brandon his phone. Brandon smiled, turning it off and putting it on the dressing table behind him.

"That's better," Brandon said, drawing Thomas's attention back to him, slowly popping the buttons on his shirt. "You spend too much time on that thing and you're never happy when you're on it."

Thomas smiled. "I can't argue with that."

Brandon unfastened the last shirt buttons, shrugged the fabric off his shoulders, and laid it on the back of the nearby chair. Thomas was silent as Brandon took a single step closer. "I'm not teasing you, Thomas. I want you to see me." He held still and then tugged at Thomas's tie, slipping it from around his neck. Then he took off his jacket and opened Thomas's shirt, adding them to the growing stack of clothing across the back of the chair.

When he turned back to Thomas, the scar on his shoulder and upper arm caught Brandon's attention. He gently traced it with his finger before leaning closer to kiss the white line of stretched skin.

"I hate that scar," Thomas whispered.

"Why?" Brandon kissed it again.

"Because it's a reminder of my biggest mistake ever."

Brandon shook his head, tracing the line with his finger. "It's a war wound."

Thomas scoffed. "Hardly."

"Wars don't just happen in the Middle East or in Vietnam. They happen every day to everyone. Wars of the heart can leave just many scars as any other kind, and they often are much harder to heal." Brandon traced the smaller marks that had to have been from the stitches that closed the wound. "How deep did he cut you?"

"Enough that I had trouble moving my arm for a year," Thomas answered, and Brandon kissed it once again. "He's gone now. They convicted him and sentenced him to a mental institution upstate. I don't have to worry about him coming back, just making sure I don't make the same mistakes."

"Because all lovers threaten and hurt you when they leave?" Brandon wondered what Thomas was getting at, but he thought he was pretty close to the bull's-eye with what Thomas must fear. His gut told him so.

"No. Because I let him get the better of me. I let him wheedle his way into my entire life, and he nearly cost me everything." Thomas turned to him. "We were supposed to spend a weekend at a cabin, and he cut me and then… I nearly bled out, it was so bad. I managed to get to a phone before I passed out." He shook his head. "I don't want to talk about this. There's nothing good that can come of it. Not now."

Brandon smoothed his hand over Thomas's shoulder, massaging. "Maybe…."

Thomas didn't pull away, but he stiffened slightly. "Why do you keep touching it?"

"Because it's a mark he put on your body, and I think this cut goes deeply enough to have reached your heart and maybe your soul. It needs to be healed." Brandon continued rubbing, placing gentle kisses on top. "I feel like you're still carrying him, and you can't. You need to truly let him go."

Thomas pulled away. "How can I? I'll carry his marks on my body forever. You don't know what else he did."

"Nope. When you're ready to tell me, I'll listen, but I don't have to know. You said he's gone and can't come back, but he's not. He's with you because you carry him inside." Brandon moved right in front of Thomas. "Let him go." Brandon gently pressed Thomas back until he lay on the mattress. "You're a fine-looking man."

Thomas shook his head. "You're the one who's incredible." He reached out and tugged Brandon closer and then down, holding him tightly. "You're young and beautiful. I'll turn forty in three weeks."

Like that was the end of line. Brandon rolled his eyes. "You need to let that crap go." He straightened up, unfastened his pants, and stepped out of them. "As long as it's there, then there isn't going to be room for someone else." Brandon worked open Thomas's slacks and tugged them off, setting them with the rest of the clothes.

"That's easier said than done."

"Yeah. I know it is. But think of what you can have when you do." Brandon inhaled deeply, knowing he needed to take his own advice. As much as he wanted his parents to accept and care for him, it wasn't going to happen.

"I can't believe we're having this conversation here," Thomas said.

"Why not? Sometimes things are easier to talk about in a strange place." Brandon climbed on the bed, straddling Thomas's body, heat radiating off him.

"You have an answer for everything, don't you?" Thomas asked as he sat up and tugged Brandon to him until there was nothing between them. Chest to chest, skin to skin, Brandon needed as much touch as he could get, and Thomas welcomingly obliged.

"Maybe." He kissed Thomas hard. "But enough talking for now." He ran his fingers through Thomas's hair. Brandon figured he'd show Thomas just what he could have when he let go. And judging by the whimpers, begging, and even the scream when Thomas tumbled over the edge, they both experienced something that neither of them was going to forget, with Brandon shocked at just how easily his own heart opened up to Thomas.

Chapter 9

"THOMAS," MARJORIE said from the doorway, interrupting his thoughts.

He looked up from his desk early Wednesday morning, still blinking a little. His head spun after yesterday's full day of work preparing for the meeting later this morning and from having his world rocked by Brandon each night since they'd arrived.

"Yes?"

"Where were you?" she asked gently as she came into the office and placed a mug of coffee on his desk.

He sighed and turned his gaze to the ceiling. Not that he expected any answers, but he needed something blank to look at so he could center his thoughts. "I don't want to be here," he finally said. "I'm ready to go back...." He could feel the business pulling him hard to New York. "This whole thing was foreseeable and avoidable." That's what made him upset.

"Probably for you. You have always had the ability to look into the future better than a damn fortune-teller. But you can't expect others to do the same. It isn't fair or realistic." Marjorie sat across from his desk and handed him a couple of the files he'd asked for. "This business needs you, it really does...."

"That's...." He sighed and set the files down, knowing what she said was right.

"But we don't need you here, physically... not all the time. At least I don't think so." She leaned forward. "Ultimately this is your decision to make." She stood at a knock at the door and left as Blaze stuck his head in.

"Can we talk?" he asked. "I'm sorry if I messed this up. I...."

Thomas tamped down his frustration. "You didn't. You got played a little bit by a greedy asshole who thought you were an easy mark."

"I'm not...," Blaze said, and Thomas knew he was about to offer an explanation.

Thomas put his hand up. "I know that." He reached for the files in front of him, but paused. He wasn't sure how he wanted to handle this, and that's what bothered him. "And you did the right thing by calling me. We need to get this straightened out, and he needs to learn that we aren't going to be messed with." He could see Blaze doubting himself, and that both irritated and bothered him.

"Thomas...." Blaze shifted in the chair.

"First thing, never apologize to me or anyone as long as you did your very best." Thomas met Blaze's gaze. "You don't owe me anything here as long as you've done that." He leaned back in his chair. "This is my fault in part. Maybe I left too soon or shouldn't have left at all. I don't know." Perhaps in his quest to get a different kind of life, he'd rushed. "We'll fix this and figure out how we move forward from here. I just don't have all the answers I want right now. Let's meet with the lawyers in an hour, okay?" He turned back to the files once Blaze had stood and left the room.

Thomas went over everything again, making sure they had all the facts. He knew he was in the right—he had all the papers that said so, and he could press it within the law—but that was going to take time and cost money.

His phone chimed with a message from Brandon. Thomas glanced at it.

Do you need anything?

A good idea. He sent the message and continued to review what he had. A knock sounded at the door. "What is it?" He was being short, but he didn't have much time.

Brandon peered inside. "Just checking that you were okay." He came in with a bottle of water. "We have everything ready for the meeting… but…." Brandon hesitated. "Marjorie has the room set up with water, coffee, even food."

"Yes…." Thomas wondered what Brandon was getting at.

"All that is to make them comfortable. Don't. Make them as uncomfortable as possible. Leave them wondering what's going to happen. Don't even put water on the table. Let them think this is quick and you're going in for the kill. At least that's what I think from what you said on the plane."

Thomas thought and smiled. "Dammit, yes. That's a perfect idea. Can you take care of that?"

"Sure." Brandon turned to leave, but Thomas stopped him. "What is it?"

"I'm not sure how I should deal with this, exactly." Thomas sighed. It was rare that he confided in anyone. Marjorie gave him a hard time sometimes, but that was her way and he liked that she wasn't intimidated by him. Maybe that was part of why he was falling for Brandon. He wasn't intimidated either.

"Okay. Why not? I bet you could do this in your sleep." Brandon smiled.

Thomas nodded. "That's what's bothering me. I'll be doing this until the day I die, or until I pack up this business and walk away."

Brandon rolled his eyes. "Sometimes we all see just the trees." He approached the desk. "You're one of the smartest, most interesting guys I know, and I believe there's no problem you can't tackle if—"

Thomas waved his hands. "Just get on with it and stop blowing smoke up my ass." He was getting more and more ramped up with each passing second. "Please just come to the point."

"Take a step back. Let Mr. Torenetti handle it."

"Blaze? But he called me for help."

"Help, yes. He didn't necessarily call you to take over. Help him handle the situation. If you need a bulldog for this, then teach him how to be one. That way he'll be able to do it next time and will know what to look for." Brandon shrugged. "You know, that whole 'teach a man to fish' thing."

"Yes." Thomas smiled as the path he wanted to take opened up in front of him. "Please go take care of the conference room and be back here by eleven. I want you and Marjorie here for the meeting. We're going to put on a show of force." He smiled, really smiled.

"You got it." Brandon whirled around and left the office as Thomas leaned back in his chair, the plan fully forming in his head.

AT ELEVEN, Thomas was still in his office. His phone rang. "Are they here?"

"Yes. They're in the conference room. There are just the two of them, Kevin Matthews and his lawyer, some sleazy guy in a cheap suit."

"Good. Get everyone else in there, including the lawyers and security as well as yourself and Brandon. Have Blaze come to my office, and we'll go in together. I want to make them wait, let them squirm and stew. I don't want anyone talking, understood? They are to go in, sit, and say nothing. Not even make introductions. I want this asshole to fidget until he's ready to shit himself. You and Brandon are to take notes. I don't care what the hell you write, just act like you're taking down every word either of them says. I want them watching and thinking about every word that crosses their lips."

"You got it." Marjorie sounded almost giddy.

Hell, Thomas felt the same way.

He ended the call, and Blaze knocked on his door a few minutes later. "You ready?" Thomas smiled at Blaze. "Just give them a chance to lay out their hand and then level both barrels at them. We know he's stalling for more money or a better offer, which he isn't going to get. Let him hem and haw, and then give it to him." Thomas checked his watch. "They've been in there for ten minutes with nearly ten people staring at them. They're going to be nervous as hell." He joined Blaze, and they headed to the conference room.

Thomas didn't smile, but was pleased when each of his people looked up from watching Matthews and his lawyer. The room was tinged with the scent of sweat and discomfort. He took his place across the table from them, with Blaze next to him.

"What's the deal, Matthews?" Blaze asked without preamble or introduction, as though the entire retinue around the table weren't there.

"I wanted to discuss some of the terms of our agreement." Matthews looked around as both Brandon and Marjorie took notes.

"You mean, the agreement that you already signed?" Blaze slid the letter of intent across the table. "The one that outlines price and timeline."

Matthews leaned to his lawyer. They spoke briefly, and then Matthews turned back, a shade paler. "That isn't the final say. It's just an outline and—"

"No. It's an agreement, binding here in New York. We have met our part of the agreement, and by refusing to meet yours, you are racking up considerable charges that go against the purchase price." Blaze was a thing of beauty, playing it exactly as they'd talked about.

"That's immaterial," the lawyer chimed in.

"No, it's not. Check paragraph eight of the agreement. Any delays caused by your client and the costs therein are to be borne by him. That includes all time resulting from preparation for this meeting, as well as research to back up our claim. It also includes all costs involved in bringing Mr. Stepford to New York, housing him, and all hours spent preparing for this little party." Blaze waved his hand. "In fact, you are paying for each person to be in this room. I suggest you talk fast and decide what you want to do. The minutes and dollars are ticking by, and you don't have a leg to stand on." He grinned. "Maybe we'll just take you to court and you can pay for all those costs as well. Paragraph nine."

Matthews grew paler and paler. "I thought we could talk about this." He turned to Thomas, and Thomas looked at Blaze, saying nothing.

Blaze stood, leaning over the table. "What you thought was that Thomas was out of town and that you could play your games and get away with them. Well, not on your life." He sat back down and adjusted his tie. "You will close as agreed, period. If there is anything more, you better closely consider the cost. Your building is already nearing a fifty-thousand-dollar price reduction, and it's only getting bigger."

Matthews opened his mouth and closed it again, like a feeding carp. He looked around the room for some sort of support.

"Are we done? Closing is scheduled for Friday morning," Blaze said. "We will do it here in this office."

Matthews nodded, shell-shocked, and his lawyer seemed about ready to slide under the table.

"Good. We'll message you with the actual price reduction tomorrow morning." Blaze stood like a lion about to catch his prey. It was gorgeous.

"We'll see you Friday," Thomas finally said, without offering his hand. "Eleven sharp."

"All right," Matthews growled, and they left the conference room, Marjorie showing him out through the office to the elevator. Only once she returned did they smile, and conversation broke out.

"You were great," Thomas told Blaze. "Thank you all."

"That was the definition of shitting bricks," Blaze said as he shook everyone's hand as they left the room. Thomas did the same, thanking them. The lawyers agreed to have everything ready for him in plenty of time, and they too left the office.

"Everyone go back to work. Marjorie, arrange for lunch for the office. They all earned it."

"THAT WAS pretty amazing," Brandon told Thomas as he took the chair next to him in the conference room to have lunch.

Blaze came in, took one look at Brandon, and did his best silent impression of Sheldon Cooper.

"You're sitting in his spot." Thomas bumped Brandon's shoulder, and thankfully Blaze took another seat.

"Are there assigned chairs?" Brandon gathered his food.

"No. Sit down," Thomas said softly before turning to Blaze. "To a great performance."

"Yeah. But we can't do that every time we run into a problem," Blaze said.

Thomas glanced around the room. "Maybe not. But you handled the problem, and next time you'll be able to do it without me. Word is going to get around quickly that you aren't a pushover, and that although I'm not here every day, they don't have room to maneuver. It's all about what others expect, and Matthews is going to be spreading the word, whether he realizes it or not, that you're a ballbuster." Thomas thought all Blaze really needed was some instilled confidence and an established reputation. He took a bite of his wrap.

"What's the plan?" Blaze asked.

"We'll stay until after the contracts are signed and then fly home." God, Thomas really was going home. Just the thought was enough to untie the knots in his stomach. He'd been back three days, and it was like he'd never left. The pressure and pace were already getting inside him, and now that he'd gotten a taste of a slower pace, he liked it. This wasn't the way he wanted to live for the rest of his life.

Brandon finished his lunch and stood, meeting Thomas's gaze for a second before leaving the conference room. Thomas wondered where he was off to, but he caught a glimpse of him at Marjorie's desk through the glass walls.

"Those two are thick as thieves," Blaze said once the door closed. "I've been wondering what they're up to."

Thomas set down the last of his wrap. "They're getting to know each other. They've been talking on the phone for weeks, so now they get to see each other in person." Thomas rolled his eyes. "Lord help us all."

The others finished their lunches and, one by one, left the conference room to go back to work.

Blaze nodded and glanced around. "What's up with you and Brandon? Is there anything going on?"

"Yes, there is. Exactly what, I'm not sure." Thomas sighed. "Brandon is wonderful and I like him, but he isn't going to stay my assistant—or anyone's—for very long. He's smart, and he watches and understands the human condition."

Blaze snorted. "What the hell does that mean?"

"It was his idea for you to do the talking. He sort of understood what was needed in the bigger picture, that you needed to be set up as the authority." Thomas leaned closer. "Brandon understands me." Just saying the words made him warm inside. "But it can't last. He's young and has his entire life ahead of him." Thomas closed his eyes. "Brandon would probably smack me for saying this, but I'm getting old… or I feel old sometimes… and he has dreams. I can't hold him back. So I'm trying to be happy for as long as I have him."

"This is so screwed up," Blaze said, and Thomas raised his eyebrows, giving Blaze a chance to explain himself. "We work so damn much that the only people we spend time with are the ones we work with. But convention tells us that we aren't supposed to get involved with them."

"Yeah… and I end up doing it twice." Thomas rubbed his shoulder, not even realizing he was doing it at first. "God, I hope I'm not making the same mistake again."

"Brandon isn't Angus. I like him. Angus was a total piece of crap and I hated him on sight. The guy was like a spider, spinning a web designed to catch your interest and snare you. It worked for a while too."

"It looks like neither of us has the best luck when it comes to our love lives."

Blaze turned to look out the conference room window. "Maybe that's going to change for you."

Thomas shrugged. "Maybe... but I can't count on it."

Blaze glared at him. "Have you seen the way he looks at you? That young man thinks you're the greatest thing since sliced bread, and don't think I haven't seen the way you look at him. Yet both of you are professional in the office. He defers to you in a way Angus never did. Brandon keeps work and your private life separate. And he's smart."

"What are you suggesting?"

"Maybe see if he's qualified to do something else? Teach him the business, make him your partner." Blaze clapped him on the shoulder. "Give him a reason to stay." Blaze stood and left the conference room without another word, giving Thomas plenty to think about.

THOMAS SANK into the sofa in the suite that evening, pulled off his tie, and sighed softly. "There's something I want to talk to you about later." He closed his eyes and wished the world could slow down just a little bit.

"Would you like me to order room service for dinner?" Brandon offered as he headed into the bedroom, most likely to change clothes. "We don't have to go anywhere if you don't want to." He sat down next to him.

"No. This is your first time in New York. Let me put on some comfortable clothes and we'll go out and see some things." Thomas left the room and returned quickly, sitting back down, leaning against Brandon's shoulder. He'd been thinking about how Brandon's talents and energy could be better used than as his assistant, and he had some ideas. Hopefully one of them would be enticing enough for Brandon to want to stay. "I can see about tickets for tomorrow night if you want to go to a show."

"Aren't a lot of them sold out already?" Brandon asked.

"Some are, but I can still see about tickets. In this town some things are all about how much you're willing to pay." Thomas patted Brandon's knee. "Give me a minute, and then you and I can head out for a few hours to have some fun." Judging by the excitement in Brandon's eyes, he'd made the right decision.

Once he'd cleaned up a little, he and Brandon rode down in the elevator. The doorman got them a taxi that took them to Times Square. Thomas hated the place. It was loud and tacky mixed with a bit of farce, but everyone should see it, and from there they could walk wherever they wanted to go.

"Jesus," Brandon breathed as they got out, his eyes wide. He turned his head to take in everything. "This place is nuts."

Thomas paid the driver, and they joined the crush of people on the sidewalk. "Yes, it is. Take a look around. There's the ball that drops on New Year's Eve and, of course, there are all the stores. That way is downtown, and the park and hotel are in that direction." Thomas pointed in those directions.

"What about some dinner?" Brandon asked, taking his arm tightly.

"All right. There are some wonderful restaurants this way." Thomas led Brandon off the square. "What sort of food do you want?" They had eaten at the hotel the last few nights.

"A burger. Something normal. All this fancy food is going to spoil me."

Thomas tightened his hold as they crossed the street with a horde of others. It was like a crush and push to move forward, and once across the street, the traffic thinned a little. He led them away from the square and down to Forty-Fourth Street. "How about good, basic steak?" When Brandon agreed, Thomas directed them to Sardi's, and they went inside.

The restaurant was quite busy and they were informed that there wasn't a table, but when Thomas handed the maître d' a fifty, one miraculously opened up. They sat down and were silently and efficiently handed their menus and had their water glasses filled.

Brandon's phone rang and he checked the screen, eyes widening before answering it. "Hello?" He listened and stood, excusing himself, as he headed for the door to step outside.

Thomas ordered appetizers when the server returned, as well as some wine for both of them. He found himself watching the door as he sat alone, wondering what was happening.

After ten minutes, the appetizers were just arriving as Brandon returned, all smiles. "That was someone from Columbia Pictures in their promotion and marketing departments. They got my inquiry, and they watched the film and saw my promotion for it and were impressed. They want me to fly out to Hollywood next week for an interview." Brandon sat down but continued bouncing.

"That's awesome." Thomas forced a smile as he shelved what he'd wanted to say to Brandon. This was what he'd really wanted. Thomas wasn't going to put obstacles in his way. Yes, what he'd come up with would have been good for Brandon and he might have liked it. But it wasn't Hollywood or his dream job. "Then there's something to celebrate." He kept a smile on his face and tried like hell to be happy for Brandon.

"I don't have the job yet. It's only an interview, but they're flying me out and they said they'd get a hotel for me and things. So they must be pretty serious." Brandon glanced down at the table. "Can I ask what that is? It looks like raw meat."

"Exactly. It's tartare. Try it on a piece of toast. It's got onion and a little egg and other things in it." Thomas spooned some on a toast point and took a bite. He loved the stuff. It was one of the food surprises he'd encountered after he moved to the city.

Brandon took a tentative bite and then fixed another. "This is good."

"Yup."

They finished the tartare and the bruschetta, which was divine. There was just enough food to take the edge off, and the waiter took their orders for dinner.

"Everything here is good. This restaurant has been here for generations." The pictures of famous stars on the walls attested to that. They were all autographed and framed. It was quite something.

Brandon ordered the filet, and Thomas did the same. He'd had it before and it was mouthwatering.

"Were they going to send you the details for next week?"

"Yeah. Mr. Salomone said they would be in touch tomorrow with all the particulars about the plane, hotel, and car service that would be there to get me. They really made it out like I'm someone special."

Thomas patted his hand. "You are. Results like the ones you got are pretty rare, and they'd be a fool not to snap you up. The entertainment business is cutthroat and as tough as it gets. What's hot today is cold tomorrow, and everyone is always hunting for the next great thing. Successful people are the ones who are able to develop the next great thing and make it something people are talking about. And that's what you did."

"It helped that it was a good movie," Brandon said.

Thomas shrugged. "It was a good movie. Not bad, but not great either. The thing was, you made it into a great movie because you got a ton of people to watch it and talk about it. That was the real success." He looked up as their salads arrived. They were huge, the way everything was in New York. Thomas was glad he was hungry, because there wasn't going to be a shortage of food.

"Thanks. So you watched the movie?"

Thomas nodded. "After you told me about it." He munched a bite of his Caesar salad, the dressing tangy, making his tongue tingle a little. "I liked it. The film was fun and had a message. It was good, like I said."

Brandon ate and talked about what the studio had told him. "They said they have a couple of positions open. It's really exciting, and when we get back, I'm going to have to call my friends to see if they had any-thing to do with this." He ate more quickly than usual, clearly excited and filled with energy.

The main courses arrived, and Thomas found his appetite wasn't what it had been a few minutes earlier. He ate his steak anyway but wasn't able to finish it.

Brandon, on the other hand, ate everything, chatting on and on through the entire meal. Thomas was grateful Brandon seemed willing to hold up both sides of the conversation, because he wasn't up for any of it. He'd known something like this was going to happen and pull Brandon away toward his dreams. Thomas had just hoped he'd have more time, that was all.

Both of them passed on dessert, and after the bill was settled, they left, wandering back toward Broadway.

"Check out the marquees and see if there's something you want to see."

"How about that?" Brandon asked, pointing to *The Phantom of the Opera*. "I've heard of that. But I think I want to look at other things."

Thomas loved the kid-in-a-candy-store vibe that rolled off Brandon. Thomas had been to much of the surrounding area, and he rarely noticed things any longer. They were all part of the city that he'd lived in for over a decade.

"You saw some of the boards in Times Square. Did anything catch your attention?"

"I've heard a lot about *Wicked*, but never saw it. The show came to Denver some years ago, but Dad wouldn't help get tickets. Now I know he was just being a jerk."

"Then let's walk that way and see what we can get for tomorrow." Thomas led the way to Sixth Avenue, and they headed uptown. The crowd thinned out somewhat as they walked. It was a great night, and once they were above Times Square, the city seemed to settle into its normal pattern. At Fifty-Second Street, they cut over to the theater.

Thomas approached the box office. "We'd like tickets for tomorrow night, the absolute best you have." He smiled, and the man showed him the theater seating chart and offered a pair of tickets in the very back. "That's all you have?"

The man looked at him as though he'd just stepped in something. "Yes, sir. The only others available are in the third row, and they're five hundred a seat."

"Then give me those," Thomas told him, and Brandon coughed from next to him. Thomas handed over his credit card, signed the slip, and took the tickets and his card back. "Sometimes I forget just how ridiculous people can be." They turned and left, heading to the street.

"You didn't have to do that," Brandon scolded. "That's a lot of money."

"No. Well, it may be, but not for this. I wasn't going to get seats way in the damn back with a pole nearby so you could spend the entire show leaning back and forth so you could see… and pay nearly two hundred a ticket for the privilege. Now we'll have good seats, and you can enjoy the show with the characters practically dancing in your lap."

"Have you been to shows before? You must have." Brandon nearly skipped as they walked toward the Avenue, where Thomas hailed a taxi.

"Of course. I took my mom and dad when they came to town. Mom wanted to see just about everything, and Dad wanted to check out the interesting bars and out-of-the-way places. They had a good time whenever they came to visit, but they were always ready to go home. This city overwhelmed them." After being gone for a while, he understood why it was overwhelming and how they felt. Maybe it was about time for him to go home too.

He finally got a taxi to stop and directed the driver to the Plaza. He paid the driver when they arrived, and together they entered the hotel. Brandon was still on some kind of high, practically dancing up the steps while Thomas followed behind, doing his best to be happy for him.

In the suite, Thomas checked his email and messages, then settled on the sofa in front of the huge television to relax. He spread out, taking off his shoes and closing his eyes. He tensed slightly when Brandon's hands caressed his shoulders before relaxing into the gentle massage.

"Holy Christ, you're wound up."

"Yeah. It was an exciting day, but they always leave me keyed up and ready for action. For years I went from situation to situation, project to project, seeing each one through to completion, dealing with problems, and pressuring people when I needed to. It's the way to get things done." Thomas sighed as Brandon dug into the muscle, forcing the damn things to relax. "Oh God."

"No wonder you are on medication and have an ulcer." Brandon continued massaging, going gently up his neck and to the back of his head. Thomas closed his eyes, and his entire body tingled as Brandon wound his fingers along his scalp. "Just let it all go. Breathe deeply and slowly, in and out. Let it all flow away." Brandon kept his voice low and soothing, and it was working. Thomas felt the relaxation and calm start to build, and soon he was half asleep. He let the worries about what was going to happen fall away, at least for now.

"Maybe I should go to bed," Thomas said, though he didn't really want to move. Brandon slowed his movements, so Thomas stayed where he was. The calm had gotten deep enough that he didn't want it to fade. Pressure, demands, disappointments, and loneliness would all make their presence known soon enough. He could wallow in a little peace and quiet for a few hours, or for as long as possible.

Eventually he got up, turned off the television that he'd been ignoring, and quietly went in to bed. After undressing, he closed the door and climbed under the crisp, plush sheets and bedding, surrounding himself in comfort, nearly falling asleep before Brandon joined him. Then and only then, he succumbed and rested.

THE SHOW was amazing, and Brandon was on the edge of his seat, laughing and keyed up through the entire thing. Thomas had already seen *Wicked* with his parents, but he enjoyed the show very much. When it let out, he and Brandon found a diner, had a late-evening snack, and then caught a cab to the hotel.

Brandon was still excited when they got back, and Thomas encouraged him to release some of that energy before falling asleep wrapped together in luxury, though Thomas wouldn't have cared if they were in a Motel 6 as long as he got to sleep with Brandon's arms around him.

Matthews came in on time on Friday, and all the transfer papers were signed and a check handed over for the purchase of the near-derelict building that was about to be torn down to make room for new development. Thomas had half expected additional trouble, but there was none, and in the end, they shook hands. Matthews left with his money… though somewhat less than he'd hoped, and Thomas had a signed and notarized deed to the property.

"Get the men to work as soon as you can get the permits. I want that eyesore down and carted away before anyone can raise an objection." Thomas and Blaze shared a smile, and then Blaze handed him the demo permits.

"Already got them."

"Then let's go." Thomas gathered the papers he needed into his case. "Send me the final architect's drawings so I can review them one more time before we file them with the city, as well as your construction plans and detailed timetables. We can review them next week." He shook Blaze's hand. "You did good. Now bring this puppy in on time and budget, and you'll be a goddamn rock star."

Blaze nodded and turned to leave. When he opened the door, Brandon passed him coming inside and started packing up Thomas's things.

"I have our bags in the empty office just down the way. The car will be here in half an hour to take us to the airport, and everything is set for when we land in Denver."

"You ready to go home, Energizer?" Blaze teased. "You've got more energy than anyone I ever met." He smiled and left the office, closing the door with a chuckle.

Brandon didn't seem to know what to do with that comment.

"If he's picking on you, it means he likes you." Thomas checked his watch and gathered the last of his things. "Let's go."

Marjorie joined them in the office. "Your driver will meet you down front and will take you to the plane, which is ready and waiting for you." She smiled and looked at each of them in turn. "You travel safely, both of you." She hugged Brandon, whispering something to him. Brandon blushed and nodded, then pulled away and left the office. "You… take it easy as much as you can, and for goodness' sake, take care of yourself." She was such a worrywart.

"I will. Give my best to Peter and the kids, and you leave the office at a reasonable time. I know you stay late because of the time difference. You don't need to. Go home and spend time with your family. Few things are so urgent that they can't wait until the following morning."

"I will if you will," she agreed, and Thomas figured what the hell and hugged her.

"By the way, there are going to be some changes around here, and I think it's time we had an office manager. I did a lot of those duties along with you, but it isn't fair for Blaze to take them on, so what do you think about taking the job? It would be a raise, and you would be in charge of all the assistants, as well as managing the office itself."

Marjorie didn't respond at first, but then she squealed with total delight. "Are you serious?"

"Yes. You'll still report to me, but your duties will change." There was nothing more thrilling than promoting great people. "Think about what you think the job should entail, and we'll talk next week. Until then, finish up here, take the rest of the day off, and you take your family out for dinner to celebrate… on me." He shook her quickly. "I have to go, but we'll talk more next week." He left his office to find Brandon weighed down with all the bags. Thomas took two of his, and they headed toward the elevator and rode down to street level. The car was indeed waiting, and soon enough they were at the airport and on their way west.

Thomas fidgeted in his seat, and Brandon leaned closer. "I…." He met Brandon's gaze and bit his lower lip. He was leaving New York, so maybe it was time to leave it all behind. "Angus…."

Brandon nodded. "Are you ready to tell me about this ex of yours whose neck I want to wring?" he asked as he got out of his seat and sat next to Thomas. "I've seen the scars he left on the outside. Now tell me about the ones he left inside."

Thomas nodded. Maybe it was time to talk about this whole thing and get it off his chest. "I've said a lot about it, but in a nutshell, Angus was hired on as an engineer. We have one on staff to help us evaluate buildings we're interested in, verify designs, and for general reference. They're an integral part of what we do. At that time I spent a lot of time working with him and Blaze."

"And you guys grew close…," Brandon prompted.

Thomas shrugged. "I don't know how it happened. As I look back, I think he was interested, I was lonely as hell, and I never thought things through."

Brandon nodded. "Are things with me like that? I know they've happened pretty fast, but do you think of me as convenient?"

Thomas thought for a split second. "No. You were never convenient." He realized what he'd said and wanted to bang his head on the table in front of him. He rolled his eyes. "I mean, things weren't like they were with Angus. He was all about staying in fancy hotels and going on expensive trips, eating trendy meals out. I think for him, the money I made was what attracted him. He wanted a lifestyle and knew I could give it to him. So he pursued me with assurances that things wouldn't affect our work, blah, blah, blah, blah." Thomas sighed. "They were all lies. It was Angus's favorite pastime." Thomas swallowed hard. "It turned out his entire life was a lie. He exaggerated his credentials and was incompetent, stamping plans instead of reviewing them properly. It nearly cost us the business. Blaze was the one to discover it. They hated each other, and thank God for Blaze's suspicions. He had his background searched and came up with a lot of crap. And I was forced to fire him, and I broke things off."

"And the scars?"

"Angus was manipulative as hell and had me buffaloed for nearly a year. He'd moved into my apartment and had taken over my social life. We did things together and had fun... at first." Thomas raised his hands. "I was in love with him. I like to think that was why I didn't see all the stuff he was pulling. After we broke up and I got him out of the apartment, he attacked me, and I know he left me hoping I'd die." The plane shook as they passed through some turbulence, and they both fastened their seat belts. "I vowed after that to never date people I worked with, and I didn't... hell, I didn't date anyone. I worked and worked. Then I moved home, and this stunning man with incredible eyes and a soul as kind and caring as I could ever hope for was hired as my assistant." He smiled and stopped the maudlin thoughts from taking over. Thomas didn't want to think about Brandon leaving.

"The last few weeks have been great." Brandon bit his lower lip. "It's only an interview. I don't know that they're going to offer me anything and…."

"None of that kind of talk at all. This is your dream, what you wanted more than anything. You go get it!" Thomas was deadly serious. "You're young and have your entire career ahead of you."

"And you're only forty and should stop talking like a senior citizen," Brandon chided.

"Thirty-nine… for six more days…." He grinned.

"The point is, you don't get to have that conversation where you tell me that it's the things I didn't do that I'll regret. My grandma already had that conversation with me." Brandon lowered his gaze but still leered at him like he was peering over an imaginary set of glasses. "I know that may be true…."

"It is true. So you have to give this your best shot. As you said, we've only known each other for—"

"We've gotten closer in the last few weeks, but I've known you a long time. Remember that." Brandon winked. "I remember you as someone who was more than fair and hired me when I needed a job." He leaned against him as the plane shook a little. "I don't intend to tank this interview or anything, but sometimes the timing on stuff is pretty shitty." Brandon took his arm, holding it.

Thomas had to agree that sometimes life's timing was pretty damned sucky, and there was nothing he could do about it. He had already made up his mind that he wasn't going to hold Brandon back or ask him to stay no matter what happened in Hollywood. Thomas was fairly certain that once they met Brandon, they were going to snap him up and make him an offer that was too good for him to pass up. Thomas needed to be ready for it.

The rest of the trip was fairly quiet. Neither of them seemed in the mood to talk, and Thomas was tired from the travel and a very busy week. He wished he could sprawl out to rest, but then he'd have had to move away from Brandon, so he sat still, just enjoying the peace, listening to the hum of the engines.

Once on the ground, they got their luggage, carried it to the car, and Thomas let Brandon drive.

"Just go to your grandma's right away. You can take care of your things and stuff." He wanted Brandon to come home with him, but he wasn't going to ask. They had spent much of the last week together and… it was for the best.

"I need to make sure everything is okay, but…." Brandon turned to him once he'd pulled to a stop at a light. "Don't think you're going to pull the 'I'm going to pull away because it's for your own good' shtick. It's been done, and it's kind of tacky." Brandon shot him a look, and Thomas held up his hands.

"I wouldn't dream of it." Thomas sighed and waited until Brandon pulled into Thelma's drive.

The lights were on and the home seemed warm and filled with life. The curtains parted and then fell back into place before Thelma opened the door.

"You're home," Thelma said happily. Thomas intended to go right home, but Thelma had other ideas and ushered him inside. "I have some dinner on the table. Travel always makes me titchy, so I figured I'd have a home-cooked meal for both of you."

Brandon went to put away his bags, and Thomas sat on a worn sofa that had probably been in the same spot since the eighties.

"Thank you."

"How was your trip?" Thelma asked. "Did the two of you get everything done that you wanted? Did you see anything in New York?"

"Grandma, it was wonderful," Brandon said as he hurried back into the room. "They got us a suite at the Plaza hotel, and that place was posh on top of elegant. The restaurant has a stained-glass ceiling that's lit from the other side. The room was as big as the whole house." Brandon sat next to him. "I was scared to sit down, everything was so nice. And we had a view of Central Park. Grandma, it was breathtaking." He held out the box of chocolates he'd bought for her. "I got these in the gift shop. Eat them slowly. They're the most expensive candy you've ever had, but they are wonderful."

Brandon was filled with energy again, and it overflowed everywhere. It was like the sun had come out in Thomas's life, at least for a little while yet. He sat back, half listening, basking in the glow and warmth that was Brandon and wondering what he was going to do without it when the time came.

"Okay." She smiled. "I take it you showed him the sights," she said to Thomas.

"He did. And he took me to a show. That was awesome." Brandon went into a recap of the trip and told her about the rest of the food. "I had tartare and it was good."

"You ate raw meat?" Thelma asked with a shudder.

"It was amazing. It tasted like beef, and there were onions and spices and it was cut into tiny cubes instead of ground, so it had texture." Brandon looked around. "It was a once-in-a-lifetime thing to be able to eat in a place like that. The women wore all these diamonds, and everything glowed and glittered, including the people. It's hard to describe. Even the elevators were extra quiet and paneled with real wood."

"Did you work while you were there or just have fun?" Thelma teased, her question setting off another recitation of some of what had happened without going into full detail.

Thomas started to wonder if Brandon had figured out how to talk without breathing, because he went on and on.

"We didn't go up in the Chrysler Building, which would have been awesome, but we were too busy." He finally took a breath, and Thelma excused herself. Brandon gave a slight grin. "I guess the Energizer Bunny came home with us."

"I guess so," Thomas said with a smile.

"Brandon, can you help me?" Thelma asked.

Thomas stood as well, gave her a hand with setting the table, and then sat down with them. Dinner was a simple herbed chicken salad, bursting with flavor.

"I'm going to California next week." Brandon bounced in his seat. "I got called for an interview with Columbia Pictures."

"Good for you. That's what you always wanted." She patted Brandon's hand, sharing a smile with him, her eyes shining.

Chapter 10

BRANDON WAS flying high. When he got off the plane from California nearly a week later, heading toward baggage claim, Thomas was at the bottom of the escalators, waiting for him.

"You made it home," he said, his huge smile filled with warmth. The few days before he left, Brandon hadn't seen that smile very often, and it had worried him. Thomas would probably never describe himself as a person who smiled a lot, but he did, if one knew what to look for, and Brandon was becoming a connoisseur of Thomas's smiles.

"Yes. It was a good trip." Brandon set his small bag on the floor and hugged Thomas tightly. "They liked what they saw. I met with a couple groups of people over a few days, and I even attended a pitch session and threw out some promotional ideas that they liked. I don't know if they're going to use them, but…." Brandon sighed and squeezed Thomas as tightly as he dared. "I'm going to find out, because they hired me. The studio wants me to come work for them. They offered me a job with a really good salary, and they want me to start work in a few weeks. They said they'd arrange and pay for temporary housing, and offered me a small relocation package, but since I don't have much, that will be great." He was so looking forward to this. It was what he'd dreamed of. But now he realized his dreams came with a price.

"I'm happy for you," Thomas said. "This is your dream, and I want it to come true for you." There was happiness in Thomas's voice, but Brandon detected a hint of sadness as well. He probably wouldn't have noticed it except that he felt it too. Even if he and Thomas could make something work long-distance, it wasn't going to be the same. Seeing Thomas every day, holding him, having him there, had become so important to him. And now there was doubt, no matter how he looked at it.

Brandon caught Thomas's gaze. "I know what you're feeling, because I feel the same way. Don't think that packing up and leaving is going to be easy, because it isn't. If it had been six weeks ago, before I saw you again, I'd have had my bags packed and been on the very next plane. Heck, before I met you, I probably would have asked someone to send me my stuff and stayed there." Brandon was kidding, but only to a degree.

"I know. Things have changed. I won't stand in your way. I can't." Thomas wiped his eyes. "We only get one life, and I don't want you to regret anything."

Leaving for the interview without Thomas had been difficult. Leaving for a job was going to be hell.

Sirens beeped and the baggage belt started. The bags slid in, and they waited for Brandon's to make an appearance.

"Everything is really different out there," Brandon said. "Sort of like New York, but with palm trees and lots of sunshine. I think I'm really going to like it." He hefted his bag off the belt and rejoined Thomas. They left the airport terminal, and Thomas motioned to a limousine parked at the curb. The driver took his bag, and they got inside. "Don't you think this is a little much for the airport?"

"You're going to need to get used to this," Thomas quipped with a smile. "The truth is that I didn't feel like driving and wanted to spend as much time with you as I can." He sighed. "I'm just trying to get my head around how things are going to change again. I-I...." Thomas stuttered, which was unusual, and worry stabbed at Brandon. "I knew you wouldn't be staying forever. You're talented enough to go anywhere. I guess I was hoping to have more time, and now...." He turned away, looking out the window. "This is what I was afraid of in the first place, but I knew.... I don't regret it. Not for a second." Thomas turned back to him. "I know you're going to go, and it's the right thing to do." Thomas took his hand, threading their fingers together. "You need to go, and I need to figure out how I'm going to move forward."

Brandon hated the thought of Thomas moving on to someone else. It roiled his gut, and the appetite he'd begun to build now that he was on the ground again slipped away. "The thought of someone else touching you makes me want to rip their throat out." Brandon had never thought he was the jealous type, but maybe that was because he'd never had someone to be jealous over before. The worst thing was that there wasn't actually someone else; it was just the idea that got him riled up.

"Do you want to know how I feel about you meeting some tanned, toned surfer guy with incredible eyes and…?" Thomas clenched his fists.

"Is this the age thing again?" Brandon pressed and then gasped and put his hand over his mouth. "Today is your birthday."

"Yes, it is, and I'd just as soon forget all about it."

Brandon lifted his bag off the floor, opened it, and pulled out a wrapped present.

"You little shit," Thomas said gently.

"I wasn't going to forget." Brandon handed Thomas the gift. "I wanted to give you something so you'd know I was always with you. I really hope you like it."

Thomas ripped open the paper with all the energy of a kid at Christmas. Brandon had always suspected that the "getting old" stuff was a façade. There was a little boy in Thomas; he simply needed to make an appearance. Brandon was happy to see him, even for just a few minutes.

The dark green paper ended up in tatters on the seat beside them, and Thomas pulled the lid off the small box.

"I thought…." Brandon bit his lip as Thomas took out a black tooled leather cuff with silver. "I found it at a store that sells all Native American items. There's an artist in Santa Fe that made this. The silver is tooled in

a pattern to represent the mountains where he lives."
Brandon took the cuff and put it on Thomas's wrist.
"You don't really have to wear it if you don't want to.
I just wanted to...."

Thomas put his hand over Brandon's as he
snapped the cuff into place. It was narrow and looked
pretty nice on Thomas's wrist. "I think it's beautiful."
He kissed Brandon gently. "Thank you."

"Happy birthday, Thomas." Brandon held him
tightly as Thomas slid his arms around Brandon's
waist and pulled him even closer. Thomas kissed him
hard and pressed him back onto the leather seat. Brandon chuckled softly. "I love that you liked your gift,
but we aren't doing this in the back of a limo. That's
just way too porno."

Thomas laughed softly. "But what if that's one
of my greatest fantasies of all time, to make out with
a hottie in the back seat of a limo?" The mischief in
Thomas's eyes was almost too much, and Brandon's
desire rose quickly. Thomas's scent and heat wrapped
around him, threatening to cut off the supply of oxygen to his brain, and his good sense right along with it.

"I think you'll get over it." Brandon put his lips
to Thomas's ear. "What if the driver looked back here,
saw us, then went into complete shock, drove off the
road, and hit some poor dog trying to make it home?
How would you feel?"

Thomas rolled his eyes. "God, you have a vivid
imagination. Where in the heck did that come from?"
He sat back up, and Brandon slid next to him, leaning
against Thomas. It was nice, soaking in his warmth.
Their joking around had cooled the mood somewhat, but heat simmered between them. Brandon was

anxious to get Thomas home so he could give him his real birthday present.

"I don't know, but I don't want the driver looking back here, seeing your bare ass, and deciding he was going to make a play for you." Brandon cupped Thomas's cheek in his hand. "I don't want anyone looking at you that way... ever." He closed his eyes, trying to keep his head from spinning. Everything seemed to be happening so fast.

Just a few weeks ago, he was desperate to find a job and his prospects for a boyfriend seemed nonexistent. Now he had been offered his dream job, the one he'd wanted for years. He also had an awesome, thoughtful boyfriend who pushed all his sexiness buttons. Brandon had actually thought of turning down the job so he could stay with Thomas, but... Thomas would probably kill him if he did that, and Brandon knew he'd probably eventually blame Thomas and regret not taking his shot.

"Sweetheart," Thomas said gently, and Brandon realized he'd been sitting there, unmoving, his hand on Thomas's cheek as he sank deeper into his thoughts.

"I'm sorry." Brandon pulled his hand away and wound his arms around Thomas, burying his face in his side.

"Don't be. You have nothing to be sorry for." Thomas ran his fingers through Brandon's hair, his hand cradling his head. "We both knew this was a possibility, and we need to face it. You have to take this job and give it everything you have. This is your dream—you only get one chance at things like this."

"How do you know you only get one?" Brandon asked.

Thomas shrugged. "Because this is how life works. Things come your way in their own time, and the important decisions in life are never easy." He swore under his breath. "I didn't mean to sound like a damn advice columnist. But... I'm not worth you giving up the rest of your life for." Thomas held him closer.

"I'm not so sure of that," Brandon said.

"I'm not. No man is. Not after knowing them for a month. It's going to hurt, I know that. But you have to go and take Hollywood by storm. It's what you were born to do."

Brandon might have gotten angry at what Thomas was telling him if it hadn't been for the hitch in his voice. This sounded just as hard for Thomas as it was for him, and Thomas was the one telling him he had to go. Brandon felt himself falling for Thomas a little more with each passing second, and it was going to be hard as hell to say goodbye in a few weeks.

"We still have some time," Brandon said around the lump in his throat. "Is there anything workwise waiting for us?"

"No. It's been quiet. You had things organized so well...." Thomas chuckled. "Including each and every meal for me laid out on the calendar in the kitchen." Thomas's belly fluttered under Brandon's wandering hand. "But I spent too much time working, so I took today off."

"Good. Because we have to go out to dinner tonight, and Grandma said I have to bring you over sometime today. Apparently she has something for you too."

"Mom and Dad have dinner planned already, and Thelma is coming as well." Thomas held him as they rode. "I was in favor of just taking you back to my place, throwing you over my shoulder, caveman-style, carrying you to the bedroom, and unwrapping you as my present, but they had other ideas."

Brandon lifted his head to look at Thomas as his body reacted to the thought of being alone with him. Even when Brandon was a teenager, Thomas had always had the ability to get him to react… and without any conscious effort. "That isn't really fair," Brandon groaned.

"I know. It seems that in their rush to give me a happy birthday, they're denying me the one thing I truly want." Thomas kissed him deeply, holding him as the car continued gliding on the freeway, closer and closer to home.

THAT EVENING, after an amazing dinner at Thomas's parents' that rivaled anything they had eaten in New York, Thomas and Brandon said good night and took his grandmother home in the limousine. She had a ball being driven around in the huge car. Not that it was a very long drive, but she had fun and had even gotten out of the car giggling and doing the royal wave to the neighbors.

Okay, maybe Grandma'd had a little too much wine.

"Let me help you inside," Brandon told her.

She shrugged him off. "I'm perfectly capable of walking into my own house and putting myself to bed. This isn't the first time I've been a little tipsy in my life, and God willing, it won't be the last." She let herself in, and Brandon waited for the lights inside to go off before getting into the limousine and riding to Thomas's, where a single light burned in the window.

Thomas got out and led Brandon up to the front door, and they went inside the large home, their footsteps echoing in the empty space.

Up the stairs and down to Thomas's room, neither of them said a thing. As soon as the door closed, Thomas kissed him, pressing Brandon back against the door as the energy and heat in the room jumped to blast-furnace levels. The panels in the door pressed into his back as Thomas cradled his cheeks in his hands, his chest firmly holding him in place. Brandon's head swam in an ocean of tingling pleasure as he reveled in the scent and warmth of Thomas. This was what he'd been missing the entire time he'd been away. Yes, he wanted the job, but he also needed this. Brandon wound his arms around Thomas's waist. There were so many things he wanted to say, and yet as soon as Thomas claimed his lips in this heated kiss, all those things flew from his head and he made no effort to try to catch them. Words were overrated, at least for right now.

"Thomas," he managed to gasp between breathless kisses, and Thomas pulled away, maneuvering him toward the bed. They both fumbled with shirt buttons and fasteners, shoes, and damn stubborn zippers that decided to be difficult. When they tumbled onto the mattress together, Brandon pawed and clutched at Thomas, needing to get all he could from him, wanting to remember each flowing muscle, every curve of his shoulder, even the exact shape of the scar on his shoulder. It was like his mind had been built as a computer for the sole purpose of memorizing every little piece of Thomas.

"I missed you...." Thomas smoothed his hands down Brandon's sides, sucking his nipples and kissing trails down his chest and belly. Being held this way made Brandon feel precious, cared for. And then Thomas took him deep, sending Brandon into a cloudy-headed daze that left him breathless and aching for more.

"You missed me?" Brandon gritted between spikes of unyielding pleasure. "What am I going to do when missing you becomes a daily occurrence?" He carded his fingers through Thomas's hair, wishing he'd never said anything, but unable to stop.

"The same thing I will," Thomas said after pulling away to kiss him. Within seconds the interruption in their lovemaking seemed like a distant memory. Dammit. All Thomas had to do was kiss him to make the world stop spinning and everything seem all right.

Thomas reached for the bedside table, and Brandon wrapped his legs around him, opening himself, needing to feel Thomas in every way possible. The cool slick raised goose bumps, and he held Thomas more tightly as his thick fingers explored, sliding into him one after the other. God, the stretch and burn were exquisite as they were replaced by Thomas pressing to him.

Brandon looked into Thomas's amazing brown eyes as his body opened for Thomas, cock sliding slowly, too slowly, but exquisitely inside his body. This was what he'd craved for today and thought about on the flight home. He needed Thomas to make love to him, just as he saw in Thomas's eyes a requited desire that rivaled his own. God, that fire burning in Thomas's eyes drove his longing exponentially.

Thomas moved slowly, rocking them back and forth, kissing and holding him as their passion threatened to burst into flames and consume them both. Each withdrawal left Brandon aching and each thrust filled him with even more desire.

"You know I love you," Thomas said softly, his movements stilling. "If you don't, then I need you to."

"Is this so I'll stay?" Thomas's cock jumped inside him, and Brandon groaned softly as he waited for Thomas's answer—one he didn't really need because he knew the truth before he even asked.

"No. You have to go. Just know when you do, you take a piece of my heart with you, one that I'll never be able to get back." He pulled away and thrust deeply once more, sending tingles of passion racing through Brandon that built until Brandon couldn't control it any longer and climaxed with such force that he gasped for breath, pulling Thomas along with him into bliss.

Chapter 11

WHO KNEW that two weeks could fly past so quickly? It seemed that Brandon had just gotten home from California, and in the blink of an eye, he was packing to leave once again. This time for good.

"I have your calendar up to date," Brandon said as he set a phone and iPad on Thomas's desk. "These are what Marjorie sent me when I first started working for you. They'll come in handy for your next assistant. I left a list of the people I've been working with. The dry cleaner and the yard service, the stores and things. There is nothing at the cleaners at the moment, and I have the house stocked with food for you." Brandon handed him a business card. "You might want to contact these guys. They're a personal chef service. They'll come in once a week and cook meals for you that can be frozen or refrigerated and heated up. It will help make sure you eat something better than takeout every night."

"I can take care of myself," Thomas said lightly.

Brandon nodded. "I know you can do anything you want. But I need to know you're eating healthy and taking care of yourself. I've also updated your calendar with doctor's appointments, and I made one for you with a dentist. Your mom helped with both of those. There are notes on your parents' birthdays and as many other things as I can think of." He blinked hard. "Marjorie said that she'd do what she can to help you until you can find another assistant here."

Thomas shook his head. "I'm not getting another one. I'll take care of the things I need myself from now on. You could never be replaced, as my assistant or in my heart." It hadn't seemed right when Marjorie asked him about it a week ago, and it still wasn't something he could do. "There's nothing for you to worry about except getting to California and starting your new life and job. I want you to call me to let me know you made it okay. If you need help with anything, you're to call. You have to promise me that." He'd worry if Brandon didn't.

This was the hardest thing Thomas had ever had to do in his life. Brandon had the opportunity of a lifetime, the same as Kornan had given Thomas all those years ago. He couldn't deny that to Brandon. He loved him too much to hold him back. But he'd moved to Colorado Springs for peace and to be close to his parents, who needed him. He couldn't abandon the people who had supported and encouraged him now that he realized how much they needed him and how important they were to his life and to the person he'd become. Up until now Thomas had always chosen what he wanted. This time he had to choose what his parents needed, even if it cost him his heart.

"I will. You know that, and maybe you can come out to visit." Brandon moved closer to Thomas's desk and walked around to stand in front of him. "I don't know what to tell you right now. I mean…."

"I know." Thomas stepped forward and hugged him tightly. "It's nearly time for you to go. Do you have everything you need?"

"Yes… no." Brandon's voice faltered. "I'll be fine." He pulled away. "My flight leaves in a few hours, and I have a car on its way to pick me up."

"What about Thelma?" Thomas knew Brandon's grandmother was going to miss him greatly. "Did you say goodbye to her?"

"Yes. I did before I left this morning." Brandon leaned against him a little more. "She didn't want me to go…."

"Thelma is strong, and the last thing she wants is for you to stay here when the bigger world is calling." Thomas hugged him tighter. "I'll stop in to see her a few times a week just to make sure she's okay. I promise."

Brandon nodded. "Thank you. I don't want her to be alone all the time."

Thomas rubbed his back for a moment, enjoying the touch. "When will your car be here? I could have taken you to the airport, you know." He stepped back, needing to put some distance between them, or he was going to want to say goodbye in a much more intimate way and there wasn't the time. They'd already said goodbye in that manner last night.

"It's best if we say goodbye here." Brandon swallowed, Thomas watching his throat work. Then he reached out, tracing Brandon's jawline with the tips of his fingers, Brandon's gaze locking on his. Damn it all, it would be so easy to ask him not to go. The word *stay* was on the tip of his tongue. He opened his mouth as the doorbell rang.

The moment was gone.

"They're here for you." Thomas turned and went to the door to let the driver inside. The driver took the luggage and carried it out, once again leaving him alone with Brandon. "Travel safely."

"I will." Brandon wound his arms around Thomas's neck, bringing them together for a gentle kiss. Then Brandon pulled back, blinking before turning. He left the house and walked to the taxi. Brandon got in and paused before closing the door to look at Thomas, standing in the doorway. Thomas took a deep breath to build some strength, the urge to race out to the taxi and ask Brandon to stay nearly overpowering. Brandon eventually pulled the door closed. The driver got in, and soon the car drove away from the house.

Thomas watched until the taxi turned the corner, and then he went inside, closing the door. He wasn't sure what he was going to do. His footsteps echoed off the marble hallway floor as though the house were empty, and in a way, it was. Thomas looked into his office but wasn't in the mood at all. He ended up in the family room, settled on the sofa, and turned on the television to find a movie. Thomas needed to fill the house with some sort of sound. The television held no interest, but he left it on before going to his office, hoping the voices would make him feel less alone.

THE DAYS seemed to meld together with little for Thomas to do other than work. He fell into old habits so easily. Just like before, work filled the time, and Thomas began thinking of projects he could develop in Colorado Springs. It wasn't New York, but there were opportunities.

Thomas drove to the grocery store ten days later, barely looking at where he was going as he assessed the area's potential for development and change. It was how he'd started in the business, and he could return to that. It would be good.

"It's a terrible idea," Blaze told him when he called to explain what he wanted as he was trying to do some shopping. The house was devoid of food, and that alone had forced Thomas out of the house and away from his computer.

"Why?" Thomas asked, taken aback enough that he stood unmoving in the middle of the produce section as people veered around him.

"Because Colorado Springs isn't New York, and I doubt they need a seven-story apartment building. They might need a shopping center or the revitalization of their historic downtown, but not a glass tower, no matter how architectural it might be."

"I'm the boss," Thomas said forcefully.

Blaze paused for two seconds. "Who cares? It's my job to make sure all projects meet our standards, the ones *you* set, and that they get done right and on time. This is a bad idea and I'm not going to green-light it. For one, it's wrong for the town—remember, I saw it when I went home with you in college—and two… you need to pull your head out of your butt, quit working yourself into the ground, and decide what the fuck you want to do."

Now it was Thomas's turn to pause. "What the hell?" Thomas's voice rose as he gripped the phone. "I can do what I want, and if I decide to pursue this, do you really think you have the balls to try to stop me?" This was turning into a pissing contest very quickly.

"Yes, I do. Mine are very nice, and they've grown and turned to brass since you visited, remember?" The humor in Blaze's voice defused the situation. "So let's stand down and stop this alpha male crap. It isn't going to get us anywhere, and besides, it isn't going to change the fact that the idea is a bad one. Or the fact that you're bored as sin."

Thomas couldn't argue with that. He looked around the grocery store and then down at himself, in sweatpants and a T-shirt. He wondered when he'd shaved last and... dammit. Thomas hated it when Blaze was right. Son of a....

"Blaze, I need to finish up grocery shopping so I don't starve and...."

"I'll let you go so you can finish what you need. I'll talk to you on the regular conference call tomorrow." Blaze ended the call, and Thomas blinked a few times to clear the weirdness from his head. He put his phone in his pocket and continued his shopping.

It seemed to take him forever because he didn't know where anything was. But in the end, he did a reasonable job and carried his purchases out to the car to drive home.

He unloaded the groceries, put everything away, and was about to get to work when the doorbell rang.

"Hello, Thomas. It's me." His mother's voice rang through the hall as he closed the refrigerator door.

"In here," he called back, and greeted her with a hug that she returned before stepping away.

"You look like hell. What's wrong with you? Are you sick?" She put her hand on his forehead. "No fever, but you look awful."

"Thanks, Mom," Thomas grumped. Everyone seemed to have an opinion about him today, including the lady making a left turn who hadn't seemed to think he was moving fast enough. "What brings you by?"

"I thought you and I could have a chat, but, honey…." She wrinkled her nose. "You're a little ripe. So go on up, shave and shower, and when you come back down, I'll have us a nice lunch ready and you and I can chat." She shooed him away, and Thomas stalked up to his room, stripped off his sweatpants, and went into the bathroom.

His mother was right—one glance in the mirror proved that. Thomas looked like hell, scruffy, his hair a mess and kind of oily-looking, beard uneven and unfashionably scruffy… and he didn't dare do that smellfy thing because he'd probably keel over from his own stink. What the hell had happened to him? The truth was, the heart and fun he'd found in things was gone. Thomas sighed, knowing he needed to pick up the pieces of his life.

With that in mind, he shaved, started the shower, and got under the hot water to wash away the stink of his own regressive failure. It was time to move forward. He just wasn't sure how he was going to do that.

Once he dried himself and dressed, he went back to the kitchen.

"That's so much better," his mom said with a smile. "Now, sit down. I made you some egg salad sandwiches." She brought a plate over to the table, then sat across from him with a cup of tea. "It's time you pissed or got off the pot," his mother began, and Thomas nearly spit egg salad all over. "You've moped around here for days, and it needs to end. So figure out what you're going to do."

"I've been looking at projects here and—"

"Not that shit," his mother interrupted. "Not work—Brandon. What are you going to do about him?" She sipped her tea. "You've been moping and grumping here for a week and a half. When I came in, you looked more like a New York bag lady than you did a successful real estate developer. You aren't happy, and you could be if you pulled your head out of your ass."

"Jeez, Mom." Thomas sat back.

"What do you expect? Brandon made you happy. When he was here, you smiled and laughed... even bathed." She rolled her eyes, and Thomas snorted derisively.

"I'm fine."

"Bull pucky. You're not fine. You can tell that to yourself all you want and it isn't going to change anything."

Thomas put up his hands in surrender. "What do you want me to do?"

She sipped her tea as if contemplating the question, which Thomas knew was an act. "Call that lovely assistant of yours and have her fire up that jet and fly out to Los Angeles. You need to figure shit out."

Thomas glared at her. "Is this you playing match-maker? Because I have one word for you—Karla. Remember?"

His mother rolled her eyes and then stood. "One little mistake and they never let you forget it for the rest of your life. What's wrong with these kids today?" She put her mug in the sink. "They can't figure any-thing out on their own, and when they get a little help, all they want to talk about is one little, atomic bomb–sized mistake." She left the room. "Make the call," she added, and then pulled the front door closed behind her, leaving Thomas alone with his lunch, wondering what the hell had just happened.

Thomas finished eating and was just contemplat-ing his next move when his phone rang. It was Marjo-rie. "What can I do for you?"

"Well… it seems you're going to LA. I called, and the pilot will have the plane ready for takeoff first thing in the morning. I also got you a room at the Bev-erly Hills Hotel. I thought that would be nice for you."

"Marjorie… what the hell?"

"Oh for God's sake. You've been miserable. I know that, and when your mother called at the but-tcrack of dawn this morning, I knew I was right, so I went ahead and got things moving."

"I'm not going to LA," Thomas said, digging in his heels.

"Now look," she snapped. "You can either sit there missing him and moping around all the time… or you can go get him. Remember that plan we had a few years ago to open a West Coast office? We even purchased a building for the expansion, which we rent out. Well, I checked and it's empty at the moment."

"So you got the idea that I should go out there and… what?"

"See him, maybe pick up on that project. Live the good life out there. I don't know—whatever you want. You've got plenty of money, and in LA there's someone missing you just as badly as you miss him."

"How do you know?" Thomas put his plate in the sink and walked through the house as he talked, his nervous energy taking over.

"How do you think? I've been talking to him. He loves his job, but he misses you, and I know you miss him, so get your butt out there, put something together that will make you happy, and get on with life." She cleared her throat. "And I'm going to go back into assistant mode instead of kick-your-ass mode. Don't make me do that again or so help me…." She was seconds away from laughing, and Thomas had to purse his lips. "Anyway. I'm sending you the details for the flight and hotel. I'm also sending you Brandon's address in LA, and I arranged for a car for you."

"Sounds like you've got everything planned out." He was feeling testy and continued prowling the house like a big cat.

"Nope. The rest is up to you." Marjorie sighed. "Do this, Thomas. You need to see him, and you need to do something. I'm not saying you need to move there if you don't want to, but you can live anywhere, and you can fly to New York from LA when you need to. You can go to Colorado to see your mom and dad or see if they want to move. But you can't just sit and mope around all the time. And he made you happy, at least I think so."

Thomas found himself nodding before he could think about it. Brandon had made him smile, and just thinking about him felt like the sun peeking out from behind the clouds. "How's he doing?"

"Good. He's already working hard, and they seem to really like his ideas. I think he can flourish there if he has someone to have his back. It's going to be tough for him alone. You know how that feels."

Thomas nodded. "Okay. Make all the final arrangements, and I'll be there. Have a car pick me up in the morning. I'm going to LA."

"Oh, thank God," Marjorie breathed. "You saved me from having to give you the speech about how love is too precious to throw away and all that. I love you and Brandon, and I really think you deserve each other, but I don't want to put myself into a diabetic coma." She chuckled.

Thomas stopped pacing and smiled. "Thank you for that. I really appreciate not having to hear that."

"Good. Now you get yourself moving and do whatever it is you think you need to do to get ready to go. I'll have the car pick you up in the morning." Even she sounded cheerful. "Call me if you need anything."

"I will. And… Marjorie? Thanks."

She scoffed. "Don't thank me. Thank your mother. She's the one who called and told me about you."

Thomas groaned. "Of course she did." Dang it, he was really going to have to have a talk with her. "Sometimes I wonder about her."

"I think your mother is amazing… and maybe a little scary. I'll send you all the arrangements." She ended the call, and Thomas shook his head, staring at his phone before hurrying upstairs to get ready to go.

Chapter 12

BRANDON'S JOB was everything he'd hoped it would be.

"I'll see you in the morning," he called as Cheryl got ready to leave the small office they shared with two other people. The studio figured proximity equaled working together—or was it forced teamwork? He wasn't sure, and it didn't really matter. He didn't have time to think about it.

"Do you have plans? I'm going out with some friends, and you could join us."

"I'm just finishing up here. They asked to have this copy done today, and I'm almost there. How about Friday?" He could reward himself for making it through a second week.

"Sounds great."

Once she left, Brandon got his head back on what he was working on. He put the finishing touches on and sent it off to his boss before shutting down his workstation and getting ready to leave. Brandon had thought that working for a studio would be glamorous, but it was work. He had seen a few people he thought were famous, but hadn't wanted to look like some hick from the sticks, so he'd paid them no attention and continued on to the office.

Brandon gathered his things and went out to the rental car the studio had gotten for him. He drove through the city on what were becoming familiar streets to Hollywood and the small furnished place they had found for him. He parked in his reserved space and went inside through the lobby to get his mail.

A man stood near the mailboxes and slowly turned around. Brandon blinked a few times to make sure he wasn't seeing things.

"Thomas?" he asked as he stepped closer, still unable to believe what his eyes were telling him. His heart beat faster as he closed the distance between them. "What are you…?"

He didn't get a chance to finish his thought. Thomas had him in his arms, kissing him hard, pressing him to the mailboxes. All Brandon could think for a split second was that he hoped to hell no one came down to get their mail because they were about to get an eyeful, but then Thomas kissed him harder and all thoughts of everybody and everything else flew from his head.

"God, I missed you." Thomas pulled away, and Brandon licked his lips, trying to catch his breath. Thomas looked great in jeans and a green polo shirt.

Brandon nodded. "Me too. Ummm, do you want to come in?" He opened the inner door, and Thomas followed him to the elevator to the third floor, then down around the hallway that overlooked the pool and to his little apartment in the back of the building. He opened the door, and Thomas stepped inside, stopping short. "I'm sorry it isn't much. I'm trying to find a place that's better, but…." Dammit, he tried to keep the embarrassment out of his voice. "How long have you been here?"

"I got in this afternoon, and I've been waiting for you to come home for an hour, I guess. I wanted to surprise you."

"You did…." Brandon set down his bag, and Thomas pulled him into his arms.

"Good. That's what I was hoping for." Thomas kissed him again.

Brandon held his shoulder, patting it gently, and Thomas pulled back. "But why? This is a long way to come for a surprise. Not that it isn't really nice." He smiled, trying to get an understanding of what was going on. Was Thomas going to leave right away, or was he here to stay? Hope warred with fear, and neither won.

"Well, for the last ten days, I think I've seen the inside of my office more than I have my bedroom. I ate everything in the house and then went to the grocery store after not having shaved or showered for three days. And every time I stopped for two seconds, I kept thinking of you."

Brandon cleared his throat. "You didn't shower for three days? What were you thinking?"

"That I was miserable. My mother came over and told me to pull my head out of my ass and come see you. Marjorie booked the plane and hotel and then told me to get out here. Blaze told me, in his own way, to quit being an ass to everyone." Thomas smiled, and Brandon molded against him. That right there was what he'd been missing.

"They pushed you to come? Is that the only reason you're here? To get them off your back?" If it was, then it was nice that Thomas had come to see him, but Brandon needed to get on with his life.

"No. I'm here because I'm going to open a West Coast office and I think I'm going to start some projects here. I realized that I need a new challenge and something special in my life. So I got on the plane and came here."

"So I'm a challenge?" Brandon pressed.

"No. You're the something special." Thomas traced his jaw with his fingers. "You're the sun that went behind a cloud the minute you drove away from the house. You weren't even there, and you were the last thing I thought of before going to bed and the first thing I looked for each morning, only to find the rest of the bed empty. That's what you are." Thomas didn't move, and Brandon didn't want to breathe in case something broke this spell between them.

"It's hard here. I don't know anyone, but I love my work. It's really cool what I'm doing, and they're happy with my work already. My boss handed me a new task to plan the promotion for a new film. It's a lower-budget piece, but I think if it can get some buzz, it could be great. This is what I've really wanted to do... and...." He realized that no matter what, things were a lot more fun when there was someone to come home to, especially someone who looked at him the way Thomas was at that exact moment, like he was the center of the universe and a damned earthquake wasn't going to shake his attention.

"I know. The guys in New York can handle almost everything, and when they can't, I have a plane. So I thought I'd look for a home out here, one with a nice yard, great view, and maybe even a cement pond." Thomas smiled, and Brandon chuckled at the *Beverly Hillbillies* reference. "Will you help me find a house and plan where everything should go?"

Brandon lowered his gaze. "Like your assistant?"

Thomas shook his head, then kissed him again. "Like my partner, the person who'll live there with me and the one who'll take up permanent residence on the other side of the bed. My only hope is that I can keep up with you."

Brandon smacked him on the shoulder. "Stop with the old-man stuff." He played with the touch of gray at Thomas's temples. "I have to worry about keeping up with you." Brandon leaned closer until their foreheads touched. "You're perfect just the way you are, and I love you like this." He stilled and Thomas shifted to the side, capturing his lips.

"I love you too." Thomas kissed him and then pulled away. The lines around Thomas's eyes smoothed out as his lips turned upward slightly and the tension slipped out of his expression. "I used to think that I had all I ever wanted and that my dreams had become reality, but I was wrong." He cupped Brandon's cheeks. "Maybe Hollywood can be the place where both our dreams come true."

Thomas kissed him again, and Brandon knew that with Thomas with him, anything was possible.

Epilogue

CHANGE WAS a good thing—at least Thomas kept telling himself that. In six months there had been plenty of it. He'd bought a house he liked on the outskirts of Beverly Hills, and he and Brandon had updated it to just the way they wanted, with clean lines and plenty of light. The house was just old enough that it had plenty of character and warmth. He'd quickly come to understand that an ultramodern home was not what he and Brandon wanted. His parents were still considering a move out, and Thomas was doing his best to convince them.

"I need to go pick up Grandma at the airport," Brandon said as he came out of the second guest room upstairs. Thomas's parents were in the small pool house, which had its own bedroom and bath, as well as its own living area. Collin was going to be in the smaller guest room, and Thelma was going to be in the bigger one, closer to them.

"Do you want me to go with you?" Thomas asked as he looked up from where he'd been answering email on his laptop. He'd originally thought he'd want a home office, but they decided against it when Thomas discovered the tranquil view of the backyard that he had from the windows in the living room. Now when he brought work home, he sat in his favorite chair and could be truly comfortable.

"You can. I got a call from your brother. His flight is expected in an hour, so I thought I'd pick them both up at once."

"Then we'd better move. That way you and I can discuss our plan of attack."

They had decided they wanted to invite Thelma to come live with them, figuring she could move into the pool house. That way she could be independent and yet be close enough that if she needed anything, they'd be right there.

"Perfect." Brandon leaned over the arm of his chair to kiss him deeply.

Thomas hugged him, and if it weren't for his laptop, he'd have pulled Brandon onto his lap. Well, that and the fact that his parents were in back with a perfect view of everything they did. "Then let's go." Thomas set his computer aside, and they went out to the garage and climbed into the Navigator for the ride.

"I was thinking that you should be the one to ask Grandma to stay. She can never say no to you about anything." Brandon bit his lower lip, and Thomas patted his leg as he pulled to a stop at Wilshire before making the turn to get to the freeway.

"I'll do that, but you should give her a few days to see how she likes it. Feel her out. She might hate it here, and you'll need to get used to that idea." Thomas intended to do what he could. He knew Brandon missed her terribly, and his parents were less than helpful, telling Thelma that she should look at retirement homes. Basically they didn't want to care for her and wanted to shut her away. It pissed Thomas off big-time.

"Okay." Brandon wrung his hands, and Thomas knew that plan was unlikely to happen. Brandon wanted this too badly.

"I know it's hard, but please be patient. Maybe ask her when she complains about your parents." Thomas smiled and Brandon nodded. That would be the perfect time and was sure to happen.

They got on the freeway, and it took a while for them to reach the airport and park. Brandon found Thelma easily enough, with plenty of hugs, and about the time they got her luggage, Thomas spied Collin in baggage claim.

"Watch out for Mom," Thomas warned as he hugged his brother. "She's already met a few people, and I swear she's lining up women for you to meet."

"Oh God," Collin said, rolling his eyes. "Not again. Tell her Karla was enough matchmaking for one lifetime." They both laughed, and once Collin had his bags, they joined Thelma and Brandon.

"Thomas, Brandon says the two of you want me to come out here," Thelma said.

"Brandon, we talked about this," Thomas chided.

"My dad is already looking at homes," Brandon said indignantly. "The big jerk. Maybe we can find a home for asshole-aholics and check him in."

"Let's let her get settled, and then she can make up her own mind," Thomas soothed, and turned to Thelma. "Yes, we want you to come out here. We have the pool house, which Mom and Dad are using for now, so you'd have your own place but would be close." He squeezed her delicate hand. "And once you sell your house, you'd have the money to do what you like."

Brandon smiled and greeted Collin, hugging him. Then he took his grandmother's arm to help her out of the airport and to the car, pointing out the palm trees and the fact that it was sixty-five degrees in late December.

"Brandon could sell sand in the desert," Collin said as they walked behind them to the car.

"He's the most caring, unselfish person I think I've ever met." Thomas watched Brandon, unable to stop the smile that crossed his lips. "Brandon makes me happy, and if he wants Thelma or half of Colorado to come out here to live, how can I say no?"

Collin stopped inside the garage, turning toward him. Thomas paused as well, and Collin shook his head. "It's good to see you in love, bro. I didn't think it would happen after that asshole, but...." He tilted his head slightly. "I should be so lucky."

"It'll happen," Thomas said as he motioned them forward. "When you least expect it." They reached the SUV, and Thomas popped open the door and helped Brandon load the luggage, and then made sure everyone was inside before exiting the lot, paying, and heading to the freeway and north toward home.

"Did you tell Santa what you wanted for Christmas?" Thelma asked from the back seat.

KEEP READING FOR AN EXCERPT FROM

FIRE AND AGATE

ANDREW GREY

CARLISLE
DEPUTIES
3

Fire and Agate

By Andrew Grey
A Carlisle Deputies Novel

When Chris Anducci is moved off jail duty and into the sheriff's office, he doesn't expect his first assignment to be protecting a witness against a human trafficking ring. Knowing the new sheriff doesn't abide screwups, Chris reluctantly agrees to work the case.

Pavle Kasun has spent the last four years of his life at the mercy of others. When an opportunity presented itself, he took it, resulting in his rescue. Now the safe houses he's placed in are being threatened and he needs protection if he is to have any sort of chance at a life.

Chris opens his home to Pavle, but he doesn't expect Pavle and his story to get under his skin... and stay there. Soon they discover they have more in common than either of them thought. Slowly Pavle comes out of his shell and Chris finds someone who touches his heart. But as the men looking for Pavle close in, they will stop at nothing to get him out of the way. But even if Chris can keep him safe, he might not be able to protect his heart if Pavle moves back home.

Chapter 1

"CHRIS," BRIGGS said as he stalked into the lock-er room like a man on a mission. His gaze was hard and his posture as rigid as a two-by-four. Anger and discontent rolled off him in waves, worse than Chris had ever seen in the month since he had moved from jail duty.

Two years of whining, demanding prisoners who thought being in jail was the worst thing to ever happen to them and thought a jail cell should be a like a suite at the Hilton. Those were the ones Chris was pretty sure were never going to see the inside of a cell again if they could help it. And then there were the repeat offenders who thought of the jail as home and a chance at three meals a day. God, he had hated every minute of the constant noise of men and women talking, fighting, yammering on about nothing just to make noise so the reality of the shit they were in didn't close in around them.

"What can I do for you?" Chris smiled as best he could. Briggs had been instrumental in getting him off jail duty and into the sheriff's office, so he owed the guy.

"It's not me. His Majesty wants to see you." Briggs turned, flashing a beam of damn near hatred out the door.

Not that Chris blamed the guy. When Sheriff Hunter had decided to retire, Briggs had stepped in as acting sheriff at Hunter's request. The entire department had been pretty happy about it. Briggs was well respected and good at his job. But the county board had other ideas. They did some lame-assed search, and lo and behold, they'd found the current sheriff, a political appointee. That had been a month ago, but Briggs still hadn't gotten over it.

"Thanks." He checked that his uniform was perfect, because that was what Sheriff Mario Vitalli liked. He was all about how things looked and appeared. It didn't seem to matter how things got done as long as he looked good—at least that was the general feeling in the locker room. "I'll go right away."

Briggs rolled his eyes. "He's on a call, so give him five minutes."

Vitalli liked everyone to wait for him, though he never wanted to wait for anyone or anything. Which would be fine if he were good at his job. He wasn't particularly—at least Chris didn't think so.

"Okay." Chris wanted to say something to Briggs. He really thought a lot of him, but everything that came to mind sounded completely lame, so he kept quiet and showed Briggs the respect he thought he deserved.

"Do you want something?" Briggs asked, taking a step closer.

Chris realized he'd sunk into his thoughts and had been looking at nothing in particular. Briggs must have thought he was staring at him. "No." Chris turned away and closed his locker. "I'll see you around." He left the room and headed up to where the big guy had his office.

The door was closed, so Chris sat in the chair outside to wait. Things had changed a lot in a month. Everyone was quiet around the office. The people who worked near the sheriff all spoke in whispers. Sheriff Vitalli didn't like noise, and to him, talking meant people weren't working. Which seemed ridiculous to Chris, because for him, talking in a sheriff's office meant work was getting done and investigations were being discussed and moving forward.

The door opened and Sheriff Vitalli tilted his head outside.

Chris snapped to his feet, went in, and closed the door. "Good morning."

"Anducci," Vitalli said, taking his seat behind the desk. Chris couldn't miss the file that sat there in front of him and wondered if he was being sent back to the jail. His stomach clenched. He'd worked hard and diligently to get out of there. "I have an assignment for you." He pushed the file off to the side as though he had made a decision. Chris wondered if it was good or bad.

"Yes, sir," he said quietly, hoping to hell he wasn't on his way back. No matter what, he was going to have to go back to his locker for an antacid.

Vitalli shook his head and scoffed. "Everyone seems to think that this office is some kind of protection service." He sneered.

Chris kept his mouth shut. It *was* their job to protect the public, which was why they became police officers in the first place. At least why Chris had. Granted, most people would think him idealistic, but so the fuck what.

"Are you listening?"

"Yes," Chris answered quickly.

"I got a request from a social worker." Vitalli yanked open a drawer and pulled out a thin file, then tossed it on the desk dramatically. "The cops in Carlisle busted up a whorehouse and found a bunch of aliens working there. In their touchy-feely world, they set about helping them and found they were brought here against their will." He rolled his eyes. "I'm not buying it, but no one asked me my opinion. Anyway, they say they need help for one person they found. It was a man, not women…." The sheriff paused as if he were expecting some sort of agreement to his ignorance and shortsightedness. He didn't seem to believe that men could be trafficked as well as women, and Chris wasn't going to agree with him.

"Human trafficking takes many forms," Chris said, then cleared his throat when the sheriff frowned deeply. "What would you like me to do?"

Vitalli groaned dramatically. "The Social Services folks found these people safe places to live, but one of them has been found out. Apparently he's preparing to testify against his captors, and now he's been getting threats. The feds, DA, and Social Services are all asking for protection for this guy, and it's falling on me to provide it. So…." He picked up the file and thrust it toward Chris. "It's you."

"Me?" He took the file and tucked it under his arm. He wasn't going to read it while standing in front of the sheriff.

"Can we not let this interfere with your shifts?" he groused, then turned back to his empty desk, grabbing the first piece of paper he could find.

"Is there anything else?"

He didn't think he was going to get an answer, but then the sheriff lifted his gaze. "Don't screw this up. It's an easy job, so just do it and be done." He turned away, back to his papers, which Chris took it as a dismissal and left the office, closing the door behind him.

With a sigh of relief, Chris went to his old metal desk at the back of the station and placed the file on the empty surface. He was usually out on patrol or working with one of the other deputies, so he spent very little time there. No pictures or papers littered the space, just a phone and a few files hanging in one of the drawers. It would be so easy for him to pack up and move on. Part of him, some fear deep inside, wondered how long he would get to stay before being sent back to jail duty.

"What did the sheriff want?" Pierre asked as he approached the desk.

"He gave me an assignment," Chris said, rather pleased.

Pierre smiled. "It looks like you're going to stay, then." Pierre had been the first one to welcome him, handing over a fresh coffee on Chris's first day. "That's good."

"Suppose so, as long as I don't mess it up." Chris opened the file and scanned through it. There wasn't much information, just a name and address for the witness, along with information on how to contact the caseworker. "Kasun, Pavle Kasun…," he said and nodded.

"Does that mean anything to you?" Pierre asked.

"Not personally. My mother's family is Serbian, and this has that sound." He picked up the phone and called the number for the caseworker. It went to voice-mail, so he left a message asking her to call back as soon as she was able.

"What did the sheriff tell you?"

"That this Pavle is a witness who was in a safe house until he was found out. I suspect he's been moved, and they want me to try to help keep him safe until the FBI and DA can talk to him and he can testify against the traffickers." It shouldn't be too difficult a job as long as they could keep his location a secret.

"Then do what you can for him." Pierre glanced at the sheriff's office, choosing his words carefully. "He doesn't think too much of others… who are different. Anyone who is different from him."

"I see." Chris knew Pierre had a partner, Jordan, who worked at the courthouse, and there were other gay men in the department. Apparently they were worried about this particular sheriff. Sheriff Hunter hadn't been prejudiced; either that or he hadn't cared as long as the job got done. Chris supposed that was probably the best kind of person to occupy the office. Someone who looked at accomplishments and results.

"No, you don't. Be careful, and do this to the best of your ability." Pierre clapped Chris on the shoulder. "Because this could be your one and only chance with this man. He doesn't seem to abide anything that makes him look bad in any way." Pierre held his gaze, and Chris nodded. They were both thinking of Graves, who the new sheriff had already demoted and relegated to patrolling country roads for speeding and crap just because one of his arrests fell through on procedural grounds.

"I know." Chris had started reviewing the file again when his phone rang. He smiled at Pierre, who left his desk, and Chris answered the call.

"Hello, this is Marie Foster returning your call. Is this in regards to Pavle?" She sounded tired, like she hadn't slept or had a break in weeks.

"Yes. I was hoping I could meet you and we could discuss what you believe is required, and then I'd like to meet him. I need to assess the situation so I can develop a plan to help keep him safe."

"Excellent. If you'd like to come to my office on Pitt Street, we can go see him from there." She gave him the address. "And please don't come in an official car. We don't want to draw attention to where he is. This is the third safe house we've housed him at, and we keep getting indications that he's been found. We don't know how, and I don't want to take any chances."

"Then I'll change into civilian clothes as well before I come see you."

"Thank you. I'll see you in about half an hour, then."

After hanging up, Chris left his desk, picking up the file to take it with him. He returned to the locker area, changed out of his uniform, and let dispatch know that he was going to be out on an assignment from the sheriff. Then he took his own car and drove the five minutes to the office.

The building embodied small and utilitarian at its worst—nothing at all of any personality in the place— and Marie's office was equally drab and stuck in the eighties. When he entered, she stood to offer her hand. Then he sat in an olive-green office chair that creaked under his weight.

Marie was a big woman with a ready smile and bright, expressive eyes that bristled with intelligence and care. She dressed professionally casual, wearing a dark blue and white blouse with jeans. Her office was as neat and organized as any he'd seen. Two phones rested in holders on her desk, which also held a computer and a few pictures.

"Why don't you tell me what's going on so I can try to help?" Chris asked, needing to get some background.

She nodded. "We discovered the house about three weeks ago, and the Carlisle Police raided the place. They discovered three people inside. Two were wanted sex offenders who are still in custody in the county prison, and Pavle, who was cowering in the corner of a closet. It took them an hour to get him to come out. Once they called me, I was able to explain enough to him that he understood those people were there to help him."

"Did you work with him?"

"Yes. I found him a safe house that was a group home with five other individuals. It was… not good. He cowered when any men came near him and basically stayed in a corner, watching everyone, for days. Either that or he went to his room and hid. I think his poor mind was simply overloaded. Then someone tried to set fire to the home and damaged it enough that everyone had to be relocated. That was hard, but then they reported people watching the next house two days after Pavle moved in." She swallowed and leaned back in her chair.

"Do you think someone is feeding his captors information?" Chris asked.

"Honestly? Yes," she said, and he nodded. "We have a system that tracks each person in our safe houses. Pavle has been anonymized, but someone is using the information to try to find him, which is a violation of a number of state and federal laws." Marie leaned forward, her demeanor turning more serious. "We can't protect him anymore, and the longer he stays in the safe house, the more he and the others there with him are in danger." She humphed softly. "At the moment he's being housed in a home for women because we didn't want to put him with men right now. And that's causing some problems for the women, though I think those are dissipating." She was clearly coming to the end of her resources. "I guess what I'm asking you is if you'd be willing to take Pavle to live with you. That way I can remove him from the system, at least as far as the information about where he's staying. Get him off the grid for a while."

That hadn't been something Chris had thought about doing, and the request surprised him. His instinct was to say no. His own home was his sanctuary, and he liked to keep it that way. Growing up, he'd moved many times—military family. Luckily, when his dad had been close to retirement, he'd been able to get posted to the Carlisle Barracks, near family. Chris's home here was like his castle because it was the first one he'd had that was his and no one else's.

"Why don't you take me to meet him and then we can see what we need to do," Chris said, purposely vague and noncommittal. Surely Marie couldn't blame him for not giving an answer until he met Pavle.

"I'll do that. But there are some things you need to know first." She floundered, seeming to be trying to figure out where to start. "We haven't gotten the full story from him about how he got here. There is a language barrier that's hard for us to breach. He does speak some English, mostly what he taught himself from listening to his captors and the few people he's been around for the last four years."

Chris gaped. How in the hell could someone live that way for such a long time? "Oh my God."

"Yes. We believe he was brought in through New Jersey during the Super Bowl in 2014. Newark is a huge human trafficking point of entry. Anyway, we aren't sure how long he's been in Carlisle or how many owners he's had over the years."

Her words sent a spike through Chris's heart. How in the hell could people do that to someone else? Chris had most definitely seen human beings at their lowest, and just when he thought he'd seen it all... *wham*... it got worse.

"Okay. So he's been traumatized and most likely gaslighted for years," he said, and Marie nodded. "So in his mind, this is all his fault, and everything that has happened to him is because of something he did."

"You got it. Years of fear and guilt conditioning. Those are the greatest weapons they have. Though, deep down, there is some steel in his back. There has to be for him to have survived this long." She gathered her purse and phone, as well as a spring jacket.

The early May weather this year had been up and down. "This is the address." She handed it to him on a small sheet of note paper, and Chris memorized it and dropped into the shredder in the corner of the office. That earned him a smile.

"I'll meet you there. I'm in the blue Edge," he explained as he left the office with Marie behind him.

Inside the car, he took a few minutes to breathe. Things like this shouldn't affect him. He saw bad things every day. But this story got under his skin, and he needed a few minutes to get his professional distance back into place. Once his anger and indignation wore down a little, he pulled out of the lot and drove to the east side of town. He parked on the street and waited for Marie before approaching the house with her.

Marie stopped at the base of the walk. "I know you're a cop, but try not to walk like one. You're standing tall and strong. I know in your job you have to project strength, but here that's not a benefit. Every one of these people have been abused or hurt at the hands of a man, so they are going to be intimidated."

Chris slumped a little and lowered his gaze slightly. "Better?"

"Try smiling and not being so serious."

Chris chuckled, and Marie must have approved because she turned, continued forward, and knocked on the door.

The house was deadly silent. Three women sat in chairs, looking up at him as though he were the devil incarnate, fear radiating off each and every one of them. He nodded to each lady and gave them all a small smile.

"This is Deputy Chris," Marie said.

"What he want?" one of the ladies asked. She had big brown eyes and her lips curled in a sneer.

"Letty, that's enough," Marie said gently, but with a firm undertone. "He's here to help Pavle."

A women bustled into the room, and Marie introduced her as the house mother, Annette.

"His room is down the hall. He rarely leaves it, even to eat," Annette explained, never raising her voice much above a whisper. "Follow me." She turned to lead him down the hallway to the last room. Annette knocked, spoke softly, and opened the door.

The curtains were drawn, the room dark, even though it was the middle of the day. A single light burned next to a twin bed that had been made to within an inch of its life, with corners sharp enough to make any drill sergeant proud. The room, however, was empty.

"Pavle, sweetheart. It's Annette," she said gently and waited.

Slowly a figure, curled up and small, made an appearance from around the side of the dresser. The first thing Chris noticed were the biggest, brownest eyes he had ever seen, filled with the pain of years of hurt. They blinked, and then Pavle stepped farther into the light. Even standing, he looked half hunched over.

"This is Deputy Chris. He's here because he's going to help keep you safe."

Pavle raised his head slightly, his black hair, long and uneven, falling to the sides of his face.

"Hello," Chris said, mimicking the soft tone the others had used. "I'm Chris. They told me you needed help, so I'm going to protect you so no one hurts you anymore." In that moment, he made up his mind to do whatever was needed to help this man, and if that meant moving him into his home to protect him, so be it.

"I'd like it if you went with Deputy Chris. He is a good man and will not hurt you," Marie explained slowly and gently.

Chris didn't expect Pavle to believe her or to agree to come. "It's okay if you don't want to," Chris said, crouching down so he was at the same level as Pavle. "This is your choice."

"Choice?" Pavle asked in a raspy voice that tore at Chris's insides, looking at him and then back to Marie.

"Yes. You can choose to stay here or go with Deputy Chris. We want you to be safe, but we aren't sure how well we can protect you here. If you go with Deputy Chris, he will protect you. Keep you safe."

"INS?" Pavle asked.

"No. He is good man. Caring. He will help you." Marie seemed to have infinite patience.

Pavle blinked, standing still, then nodded and walked to Chris. It seemed as though he either didn't understand or thought he didn't have a choice, even though he was being given one. Chris held out his hands, palms up, to show that he wasn't going to hit him. When Pavle looked at him with those huge eyes and the face of an angel, he looked much younger than the twenty-four listed in his file. Maybe that was his previous owner's fetish. Still, after all he'd been through, Pavle's handsomeness and light shone through, with soft features and an almost delicate frame.

"I'll gather his few things," Annette said.

Marie extended her hand to take Pavle's gently. He went with her in silence. She led him out of the house, and once they were in the sun, Chris got a better look at him. Pavle was pale, probably from years of being inside. Chris reminded himself to ask Marie about any past injuries. He suspected that Pavle had been treated very badly in the past and he needed to know if he was okay physically.

"Thank you for doing this," Marie said once she had opened the door to Chris's car and gotten Pavle settled in the passenger seat. He sat without moving or looking to either side. "You have to keep him safe. He is the main witness against the man who held him for nearly two years. We need to get that man and then trace back to the people who sold Pavle to him. We're pulling each thread to see what we can unravel."

"Okay. I will do my best, I promise you."

"I'll follow you to your house and help Pavle get settled."

As Marie got to her car, Pavle reacted for the first time.

"She's just riding separately. She will be back in a few minutes."

Chris drove the short distance to his house and pulled into the garage. He didn't want Pavle to be seen, and yet he also didn't want him to feel like a prisoner again by being hidden. He got out and waited, hoping Pavle would get out on his own. After a few moments, Pavle opened the door and climbed out of the car. Chris opened the door to the yard and motioned for Pavle to go ahead of him.

Marie came through behind him, and Chris closed the garage doors and joined the two of them in the yard. Pavle looked around, saying nothing. Chris wished he would say something… anything. He was way too quiet, and that worried Chris because he had no idea what he was thinking, and damn it all, those eyes still held buckets of fear.

"It's okay. This is where you are going to stay." Marie gently coaxed Pavle toward the house, and he shuffled along, looking at the yard. Hopefully he liked what he saw. Chris had spent too many hours working out stress for the garden to be unappreciated.

Chris opened the back door, went inside, and turned on lights, letting Marie bring Pavle in the kitchen, motioning toward the living room. Maybe this was the biggest mistake of his life. He wasn't equipped to handle someone as fragile and frightened as Pavle. Chris had no clue what he needed or even how to get through to him.

"I sold?" Pavle finally asked barely above a whisper.

Chris caught Marie's gaze, and his heart twisted in his chest. God, this was going to wrench his guts six ways from Sunday.

"No. This is where you are going to live. You are not going to be sold to anyone anymore. Deputy Chris is here to help you and nothing more." She patted his hand and took Pavle through to the other room.

Chris got three glasses of water and put some cookies on a plate. He needed some sugar if he was going to get through this in one piece.

Marie and Pavle were talking softly on the sofa when Chris handed each of them a glass and offered them cookies. Marie took one, and Pavle stared at the plate as though it were a foreign object. Finally, he took one and ate a small bite before shoving the whole thing in his mouth, chewing and swallowing like he hadn't eaten in days, then he drank the entire glass of water.

Chris offered him another, and Pavle took it in disbelief, ate it quickly, and then rested his hands in his lap.

"Why don't I take you upstairs and show you your room?" Chris offered. He led Pavle and Marie upstairs and into the bright guest room, with cream walls and a deep green coverlet on the bed. The furniture was white and rather plain, but functional. He'd found the set at a secondhand store and painted it himself to clean it up. "You can put your clothes in here," Chris told Pavle, who shrugged and looked down at what he was wearing.

"I have his things in the car. There isn't much right now," Marie explained.

"That's okay. I can take him to get everything he needs." Chris needed to do some shopping tomorrow anyway and figured he could take Pavle with him. He would need to disguise Pavle somehow. "I have something he can wear tonight if he needs to, and then we'll shop tomorrow."

"Thank you," Marie said with a sigh. "Are you going to be okay?" she asked Pavle, who nodded.

Chris showed her downstairs, while Pavle stayed behind, and got Pavle's things from her car.

"I'll stop by whenever I can. He's going to need care and plenty of help."

"Of course. Is he seeing a counselor?" Chris asked.

"Yes. But they are having some language issues. I'm working on it. I'd like to find one who understands

Serbian so they can talk in his native language, but it's very difficult in this area. But I'm not giving up. I'll let you know when his next appointment is." She left through the back gate, and Chris locked it from the inside and went back into the house. He brought Pavle's things up to his room and set them on the bed next to him.

"Are you hungry?" Chris asked. When Pavle finally nodded, Chris motioned, and they left the room. He didn't know what to make for dinner, but decided on pasta. He got Pavle seated in the kitchen and started cooking. It wasn't fancy, and the sauce was from a jar, but when he put the plate and glass of water in front of Pavle, the surprised expression and then the way he shoveled the food into his mouth, his arm nearly a blur, told him a great deal about Pavle's treatment. Chris got his attention and ate slowly. "I'm not going to take your food."

Pavle nodded and ate a little more leisurely, but his body was rigid the entire time, as if he expected Chris to take away his plate at any moment.

Once Pavle had eaten everything, Chris got him a little more and showed Pavle what he had to drink. Pavle pointed, and Chris poured him some juice. Pavle sniffed the glass and sipped before downing the liquid like it was a huge shot.

"I am not going to take your food or drink. You can have all you want." He poured Pavle some more grape juice and set it in front of him before clearing the dishes. Pavle stared at the glass like it held some deep meaning and then sighed dramatically and drank it.

Once Chris had cleaned up, he motioned for Pavle to follow him through to the living room. Chris put on the television and sat in the chair. Pavle sat in the other one, alternately watching the television and then him. It was a little unnerving, but Chris sat still and tried to relax, hoping Pavle would do the same.

At bedtime, he turned off the television and led Pavle up the stairs, turning out the lights. "It's time to go to bed." He showed Pavle the bathroom and the towels that were his to use. He also found a new toothbrush and some extra toiletries for him, placing them on the bathroom counter. He tried to think of anything he was forgetting. "Is there anything else you need?"

Pavle shook his head and went to his room, and when Chris came in to bring him some pajamas, Pavle stood in the center of the room, naked, his hands behind his back, head bent down.

ANDREW GREY is the author of over 100 works of Contemporary Gay Romantic fiction. After twenty-seven years in corporate America, he has now settled down in Central Pennsylvania with his husband, Dominic, and his laptop. An interesting ménage. Andrew grew up in western Michigan with a father who loved to tell stories and a mother who loved to read them. Since then he has lived throughout the country and traveled throughout the world. He is a recipient of the RWA Centennial Award, has a master's degree from the University of Wisconsin-Milwaukee, and now writes full-time. Andrew's hobbies include collecting antiques, gardening, and leaving his dirty dishes anywhere but in the sink (particularly when writing). He considers himself blessed with an accepting family, fantastic friends, and the world's most supportive and loving partner. Andrew currently lives in beautiful, historic Carlisle, Pennsylvania.

Email: andrewgrey@comcast.net

Website: www.andrewgreybooks.com

FIRE AND WATER

ANDREW GREY

CARLISLE
COPS
1

Carlisle Cops: Book One

Officer Red Markham knows about the ugly side of life after a car accident left him scarred and his parents dead. His job policing the streets of Carlisle, PA, only adds to the ugliness, and lately, drug overdoses have been on the rise. One afternoon, Red is dispatched to the local Y for a drowning accident involving a child. Arriving on site, he finds the boy rescued by lifeguard Terry Baumgartner. Of course, Red isn't surprised when gorgeous Terry won't give him and his ugly mug the time of day.

Overhearing one of the officers comment about him being shallow opens Terry's eyes. Maybe he isn't as kindhearted as he always thought. His friend Julie suggests he help those less fortunate by delivering food to the elderly. On his route he meets outspoken Margie, a woman who says what's on her mind. Turns out, she's Officer Red's aunt.

Red's and Terry's worlds collide as Red tries to track the source of the drugs and protect Terry from an ex-boyfriend who won't take no for an answer. Together they might discover a chance for more than they expected—if they can see beyond what's on the surface.

www. dreamspinnerpress.com

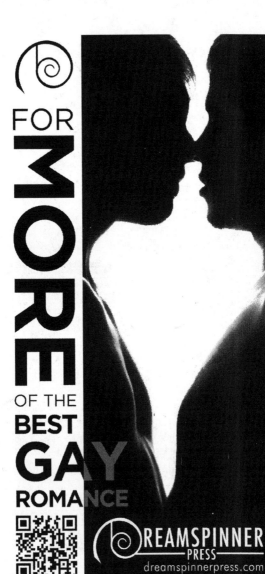